CW00871891

THE TRUSTING RUSTIC

J.C. Crockett

MINERVA PRESS
LONDON
ATLANTA MONTREUX SYDNEY

THE TRUSTING RUSTIC

ISBN 1 86106 965 0

First Published 1998 by
MINERVA PRESS
195 Knightsbridge
London SW7 1RE

Printed in Great Britain for Minerva Press

THE TRUSTING RUSTIC

Physiognomy is not a rule given to us to judge of the character of men; it may enable us to make a conjecture.

La Bruyère

Contents

Chapter One

Introductions

The countryside mirrored the mood of Calico. It was shaking off its winter mantle; allowing brave budded shoots to burrow up through the hard earth. Fighting for their chance of survival determined to herald the wake of spring. Calico, watching from the bus window, took in the scene conveying fresh courage to her. *All starting out anew*, she thought. *The wayside flowers have less idea what is before them than I have whatever greets them rain, hail, wind, frost, snow, or sunshine, they challenge and stand erect with upturned faces.* Reminding Calico of a saying on a sampler at home: 'turn your face always towards the sun and the shadows will fall behind.'

Calico tried to appear relaxed, to give an air of self-assurance about her, as if she was a well-travelled person; when in fact this was only her second time on the bus to her nearest big city. (The bus conductor effectively deflated her image by offering her the end of his roll of tickets, which he gave to youngsters when he changed to a new roll). She was seventeen. Her hairstyle had not altered since she was twelve; she wore her long dark hair straight and severe. No powder masked her pale complexion. No hint of colour on her eyelids, or mascara on her long lashes to accentuate her liquid brown eyes. No smear of lipstick to emphasise her full pouting lips. Though unaware of this yet (for she had not been initiated into the Art of Womanhood); her face if skilfully made-up, was the sort of face that sent a stab of half-pain, half-pleasure coursing through a man when turned on him to full effect. A face that countless women have and use to their advantage; as any history book will verify.

Calico contemplated what lay in store for her. She had been accepted, after a nerve-racking interview, as a parlourmaid at the Lord Mayor's Mansion House at Brydle. What sort of people would she meet? Would they be so different from the country folk she had been surrounded by all her life, on the farm? She knew she would have to be on her guard, she was not sure against what though. Her mother had warned her to tread carefully. 'City folk are not like country folk,' her mother had said, 'they have different ways.' But she never went into detail what the different ways were, intimating she had said enough and covered all eventualities in that single simple statement. Leaving Calico no wiser but more watchful.

She would miss her family very much, she thought. Her gran was always recounting tales of bygone days, when they used horses instead of tractors on the farm. The steady pace of life, working from dawn till dusk. Dozens of farmworkers standing shoulder to shoulder in the hayfields, the cornfields, and the rootcrop fields. Being able to chat to each other with some friendly ribbing, building up a camaraderie between them. Then, with the advent of noisy machinery, there were fewer workers needed, no time to chat, and difficult to make yourself heard above the belching, belligerent, menacing, mechanical menagerie the farmers introduced to save themselves labour costs. The old, friendly, calm, unhurried way of life faded, the new, noisy, stressful, every-man-for-himself way of life took over. 'Even the weather,' Gran would remark, 'has changed. The days seemed sunny for weeks on end over the haymaking time. Now we're lucky if we get two fine weeks together.' Then Gran would recall her working day. 'We'd start out as the sun was climbing the sky. Watching the beauty of it, a personal painting God had created that morning 'specially for us, for every sunrise differs, seemed to inspire us for the labour that lay ahead, working along with Nature that was all around us. The odour of the drying grass, so sweet a perfume, met us long before the hayfield was in view. We'd collect our pitchforks from the cartshed and work steadily till breakfast time. The farmer, having finished the milking by then, would fetch us out cold tea and a round of bread and dripping each. Then we worked through till it was time to eat the food we brought with us; usually a hunk of bread and cheese or ham, or maybe a jam sandwich. Some snatched forty winks in the shade of the trees. We were brought some home-brewed scrumpy when the farmer left us to go and do the second milking. We went home when it got dusk, had supper, and fell into bed ready for the next day.'

Calico thought perhaps it was no bad thing that days were cut to eight hour ones now, but the way her gran described the old days, she made them sound idyllic. There was no mention of the exhaustion, the sweating brows, the aching limbs, Calico noticed. Pain is something you only feel at the time and fades in the memory, pleasure remains in the memory and is lasting.

Calico turned her thoughts to the livestock back at the farm, she even began to feel sentimental about them. The docile cows with their big brown eyes and flirty lashes. The contented pigs snuffling and grunting, foraging for food. The busy hens scratching and scrabbling in the dirt for an odd morsel. The noisy geese and the evil-tempered gander. And her beloved pets, her two long-coated German Shepherd bitches. Liaka, black and silver (grey) and Leonie, black and gold. It was difficult saying goodbye to her dogs. They could not understand why she was leaving them.

Dogs have an undying devotion to their owners and never leave their side. They cannot be expected to comprehend how their owners could ever leave them. Liaka was two years old, and though she thought a lot of her, there was a special bond between Calico and Leonie, having virtually grown up together, and roamed freely around the farm at each other's side. Calico could imagine Leonie sitting waiting patiently, head on paws, sad brown eyes fixed on the gate her beloved mistress would return through. At least they had each other for company. Calico liked to see at least two of everything, as an only child, she knew what it was like not to have a soulmate. Though she was never really lonely, she always felt there was something missing in her life through her childhood years.

The countryside and the sprawling suburbs of the city were now merging. Soon there would be nothing to see from the bus window but tightly packed houses, until it reached the larger city dwellings that had more character and history to them. Then on past the shopping centre, the bus slowly edging its way through the traffic towards its depot and disembarking. *How many times it must have made this journey*, thought Calico, *carrying passengers to a happy or tragic event. Not knowing or caring what happened to them after they reached their destination. Doing its duty, doing only what was asked of it, as a lot of people do only what is asked of them and never contribute more to society*. The bus pulled into the bus station. Calico collected her belongings together, struggling with her suitcase, expecting at least one offer of help but receiving none. *Oh well!* she thought, *I really am on my own now I've left the helping hands at home*. She dismounted from the bus with difficulty. Already beginning to feel homesick; even though home was only twenty-five miles away.

Calico made her way to the taxi-rank. She felt so alone, not knowing anyone among the head-down determined knowing-where-they-were-going people in the streets, rushing past her without a second glance. It's hard to adjust, when you know, or are known by, every person in the village you grew up in, to a big city where no one gives you the time of day unless you are likely to be of some use to them. Even taking a taxi was a new experience for Calico, but it was easier than trying to get there on an inter-city bus with her heavy suitcases. The Lord Mayor's residence was positioned at the opposite end of the city, on the outskirts near the Downs, too far to walk with luggage. She had reasoned this out when she attended the interview, justifying to herself that the expense of a taxi was necessary.

It seemed that one queued in front of the taxi-rank sign, and the taxis picked people up in an orderly fashion. This was not at all what Calico had been expecting. Seeing films of people running and jumping straight into taxis, announcing their destination and being whisked away, leaving some open-mouthed annoyed individual, who had been patiently waiting on the pavement, scowling after them. This had been a vision that had worried Calico. Not being pushy, she imagined herself standing waiting on the pavement an inordinately long time. Therefore she was relieved to find such a civilised arrangement, and got into a taxi when her turn came quite thankfully. The taxi-driver put her cases in the boot and returned to his seat. 'Where to Miss?' he asked.

'The Mansion House please,' Calico replied importantly. It did sound grand.

'Righto missy, will do,' he reiterated. 'The Lord Mayor's, now ain't that grand, thee bin asked fer tea?'

Calico, thinking it none of his business but not wishing to appear impolite, answered him. 'No, I'm not going there for tea.' Surely he would leave the matter at that. But no, she had underestimated the tenacity of taxi-drivers who like to know what is going on in their city.

'Thee must be workin' there then,' he assumed.

'Yes,' Calico replied, curtly. Is this what her mother meant about city folk being different from country folk; who did not ask forthright questions, but waited for you to proffer information? 'Mind your own business and mind it well' was an old country saying.

'Doin' what?' he persisted.

'Parlourmaid, and I've already passed the interview. I didn't know I had more to pass with anyone I met on the way,' she replied, testily. Why should she continue to be polite to this man when he was so nosy?

'There's no need fer thee t'be so uppity Missy. Thee wages be paid by the ratepayers and I be one o' they. So I 'ave a right to know 'ow me money's bein' spent and on who. They'm ferever changin' parlourmaids up at thik thar Mansion 'ouse. Makes I wonder why?' he retorted quickly but not unpleasantly. ''Ere be Miss jarney's end.'

Calico had been dreading this moment, but it was preferable to staying in the taxi with this obnoxious man. Telling her he was practically paying her wages, and that all the ratepayers of the city were her bosses. It made her position, which up until then she had thought of as an achievement, seem menial. She knew he was right. He only put into words what she herself would have realised, if she had thought about it at all. This made her dislike him even more. Although people often say they are in favour of plain speaking, they seldom are when it is directed at themselves. Calico did not give him a tip. She told him that if he was paying her wages, then there was not any point in her giving him money that she would indirectly receive back. She would keep it and cut out the middle man. To which, surprisingly, the taxi-driver had no immediate reply. He just stared at her, then the corners of his lips twitched and a smile spread. As he was driving out he wound down the car window and shouted back to Calico. 'Thee'll do fer I missy,

I'll warrant thee'll last longer than t'other'uns did. Thas if thee's a mind to.'

Here she was then, embarking on her working life. Whatever she did from now on would shape the pattern of her future. Her life had become her responsibility. Calico stood on the threshold of the door. *One step forward and I'm not a child any more. I'm a responsible adult, a wage-earner*, Calico said to herself. *One step forward and there is no going back.* If we had any conception what lay ahead of us in life, I doubt if many of us would have made such a great effort to leave the sanctuary of the womb; let alone step over the threshold between childhood and adulthood eagerly.

At this moment, while Calico was still pondering the enormity of the step before her, Mr Rolph, the head butler appeared to welcome her; which made an ironical picture: Calico, pure and innocent, as yet unsullied, waiting for life's canvas to be unravelled in front of her in pristine condition; Mr Rolph, nearing the end of life's canvas, which he had thoroughly despoiled and stained with greed and lust. It was like the spider and the fly, the serpent and Eve, the devil and the Virgin Mary. It could have been a painting from the Renaissance. The eternal good contrasted with evil. The continual fight. Even though it was mild outside and struggling sunbeams made the day bright, the corridor leading to the kitchen, down which Mr Rolph led Calico, was dark, cold and gloomy. Calico shivered slightly, feeling the hairs move on her arms where goosepimples had sprung up. A sense of foreboding, which Calico mistakenly took to be nervousness at meeting strangers, welled up within her.

So many new faces, seated around the table, smiling a welcome at her, as she entered the kitchen with Mr Rolph.

'Hello dear,' said a thin-faced wiry-haired woman. 'Timed that right. Sit down an' I'll pour you a cup of tea. We've just this minute started our tea-break.'

'That is the kind of remark you will get used to, from Olive, she is the cook, according to her they have always "just started their tea-break". Next to her is Amy, another parlourmaid; three of the cleaners, Susan, Vera, and Grace; and the gardener. You will meet the housekeeper, the under-butler, the third parlourmaid, the other cleaner, and the chauffeur, later. This is our new parlourmaid, Calico,' said Mr Rolph, introducing her to everybody.

Calico sat in the chair indicated by Olive, and more questions started. She answered them as best she could, without giving away more information than she thought was necessary. She was quite relieved when Olive decided the break was over, and they all went back to their various jobs.

Mr Rolph had instructed the under-butler to take Calico's suitcases up to her room, while she was drinking her tea. Mr Rolph took her up the backstairs to her room. He explained that all the staff used the backstairs to all the floors. The main staircase was for the Lord Mayor; her husband, who was referred to as consort; and their guests. Though this was modern times, they still liked to maintain the etiquette as it used to be. The staff had the use of the basement, which consisted of the main kitchen, the staff dining room and the staff sitting room. The ground floor and first floor were the Lord Mayor's quarters. The second floor contained the bedrooms and bathroom for the live-in staff.

Mr Rolph opened the door to her room, and stood back to let her enter first, (ever appearing to be the gentleman, but how deceiving outward appearances can be.) The room was large, airy, and a little shabby. It had a well-worn look about it. The bedroom suite was heavy, old-fashioned, walnut and marble, and the washstand still had a floral-patterned set of jug, basin and soapdish displayed upon it, with the chamberpots on the shelf underneath. Mr Rolph went over to the bed. He looked at Calico meaningfully and remarked, 'I know this bed is comfortable, my dear.'

Calico, inexperienced and unable to read the expression in his eyes, moved over to look out of the window. 'What a view of the city from up here, and there's a balcony,' she said quickly, too quickly.

Mr Rolph, catching the uneasy tone in her voice, sensed that with this one he would have to tread carefully. He could tell after the first meeting with a woman, how to treat her to get what he wanted, he boasted to himself. Years of experience enabled him to categorise them. Each category had to be handled differently. Some gently with kid gloves, wooed and charmed; some roughly, brusquely, with indifference; some a combination of both. He could be a real tough he-man, or a simpering idiot at their feet. He did not mind what role he played, as long as he always got his prize at the end of the display. Mr Rolph was a good-looking man for his sixty-five years. He still had a full head of hair, greying in a distinguished way. Tall and still youthfully slim, he cut a fine figure that many younger men would envy. But there was something in his eyes, that you could see, if you looked too closely; you could see the lust, the greed, the selfish pleasures he needed to satisfy his appetite. You could see ruin and heartache. You could have seen all this; but when Mr Rolph made love, he kept his eyes closed the whole time. 'I will leave you to unpack your suitcases and freshen up. Then come downstairs, I will get someone to show you around the house, and find you a uniform.' Mr Rolph said, in a business-like manner, bringing them both back to an employer/employee status, so that Calico would think she had imagined the look in his eyes, and mis-read the situation. Calico was relieved. She was wrong, he was just being friendly, there was nothing to worry about. So she fell for his ruse, as Mr Rolph knew she must. Being young and naive, she would explain it away to herself, and forget the incident. Which was why Mr Rolph smiled to himself, as he closed the door on his way out. Calico on the other side, sat on the bed and surveyed her surroundings. *Well*, she said to herself, *this is now my temporary home.*

What a journey into the unknown life is, Calico mused, as she started to unpack. *How fortunate are those few who know exactly what they want from life, and can say at the end of it, 'I have no regrets, I made no mistakes, I took no wrong turning, I was in control all my life.'* Calico knew she would not be one of the fortunate. She had no direct aim in view. She had applied for many posts, this just happened to be the one that she had gained. She had read somewhere that life was like a giant tapestry. We weave our own threads, which intertwine with others along the way, and cannot be unravelled once woven. Calico preferred to think it resembled more a piece of patchwork, with the colours of the patches ordained by the phase you were going through. Like Picasso with his blue period and his rose period.

How difficult life was. She remembered her friend Charlie from her home village, was always saying to someone, 'Go on young 'un, take a chance,' when they were dithering over a certain matter. Calico understood what he meant, all anyone was able to do was 'take a chance' on life, and hope they took the right chances when they came their way. Living isn't for the faint-hearted. People must be strong, for not many opted out before their time was up, whatever burden was put upon them. Calico could only recall one person she vaguely knew, who had committed suicide. *What morbid thoughts!* Calico brought herself out of her reverie, finished unpacking, brushed her hair, and made her way downstairs to find out about her duties and so on.

Calico entered the kitchen.

'Hello, I've been waiting for you. I'm Amy,' said a girl, approaching her, 'Mr Rolph asked me to show you around, and explain your duties, seeing as it's my afternoon to work. We parlourmaids work on a split-shift system, to cover from seven in the morning to ten at night, seven days a week. We get one and a half days off a week, except every third week when we get the weekend off. We have to launder our own uniform, and starch the caps and aprons. Blue long-sleeved dress and plain apron and cap for mornings. Maroon long-sleeved dress with detachable white lace collar and cuffs, and fancy apron and cap, for afternoons and evenings. And black or brown shoes. That's the only time Mr Rolph is staid and old-fashioned. He sticks rigidly to the traditional rules of dress, likes to see everyone properly turned out. I wore a pair of bright red courts with my afternoon uniform once, 'cos I was going out that night, and I wanted to break them in by wearing them for a while. He happened to catch me, gave me a long lecture on the expected behaviour and attitude of persons working for the Mayoral Establishment. How pomp and circumstance had made our nation great. Then he goes into his Lord Kitchener's speech: "Discipline, discipline, discipline... that is the one thing needful." Tells me, it was the discipline amongst our armed services that won the war. I suppose if some had worn bright red boots, we'd be under German rule by now. Mr Rolph always refers everything back to the war. He was a Navy man and he enjoyed his time in service. I don't know what the people of our generation are going to find to talk about when they get older. They won't have a war to harp on about and re-live with each other, like Mr Rolph and his cronies.' As Amy was talking they made their way up the back stairs to the first floor. 'We aren't supposed to come up here, when there's no one about in the afternoon. Mr Rolph gave me permission to show you around the first floor, but he told me to leave the second floor until tomorrow morning.'

They entered the entrance hall. Calico looked around her in amazement. It was so richly furnished. An elaborate clock, with carved figures at each corner, was striking the quarter hour. It centred on the mantelpiece of an ornate marble fireplace, surrounded by delicate porcelain figurines and colourful Venetian glassware, with two large, rather ugly vases book-ending them all. Small rosewood half-circle side tables, with marble busts resting on them, were placed against the walls. Above these were large dark oil paintings in gilded frames. A big brass dinner gong stood in the corner nearest the door to the back stairs. Rays of sunlight filtering through the stained glass panels of the oak front door, left a kaleidoscope of coloured images across the Oriental carpet that covered the floor. A crystal chandelier twinkled above the scene, reproducing the sun's stained rays further, and enhancing the decorative ceiling.

Calico was surprised. She had not expected such opulence. She had visited several local stately homes, that were open to the public, where this entrance hall would not have been out of place.

Amy opened the door to the left, and they entered a large room, just as lavishly furnished as the entrance hall had been. 'This is the Mayoral reception room or parlour,' Amy informed her, 'where the Mayor receives her visitors before a formal banquet, and where she holds a coffee morning every first Wednesday of the month.'

The room was light and airy, due to the huge bay windows at either end of it. This room too had several oil paintings, but it was the furniture which attracted attention. Elaborately carved ebony cabinets depicting miniature scenes; mahogany bookcases with leaded glass doors, filled with leather-bound tomes; a grand piano; a selection of unusually-shaped antique chairs; a leather-topped partners' desk; and towering above them all, in the corner, a magnificent grandfather clock. A unique specimen made by local craftsmen, commissioned by the wealthy merchant, who had the Mansion House built for himself, and then willed it on to the City of Brydle, having no near kin.

They re-entered the entrance hall, and took the door which led into the middle room. This room was more simply furnished, being mainly functional. A drinks cabinet filled one wall, and a snooker table was in the centre of the room.

'Which,' Amy explained, 'is covered with a large board, and used as a base to serve the food and drink from, when there is a banquet in the adjacent dining room.'

The prepared food reached the room by means of a dumb waiter; a small lift that travelled between the kitchen and this room. It was used for transporting food on the way up, and dirty dishes on the way down. There were three doors to this room to make for easy access. They left the room by the door that led to the adjoining dining room. A highly-polished, richly-coloured, mahogany table, seemed to dwarf the room, surrounded by matching chairs, with tapestry seats. A sizeable carved sideboard with brass decorations, took up one wall. This was used to store the silver cutlery, silver serving dishes, silver cruets, and so on. Also the bone china services, the crystal glassware, and the starched table linen.

'There's more silver tableware,' said Amy, 'solid silver candelabras, candlesticks, and salvers. And a solid gold engraved salver, worth a fortune. They only come out for special banquets. They're kept under lock and key in a walk-in safe. The butlers look after them, they have to clean and polish them in the safe-room. What do you think of the place, then, posh isn't it?'

'I should say,' Calico answered, 'I don't know what I expected really, but I wouldn't have imagined such a grand place as this. Everything looks so expensive, the furniture, the paintings, the sculptures, the ornaments, the floor coverings; who owns all this?'

'The City Corporation sort of keep it in trust,' Amy informed her, 'no one actually owns it, I don't think so anyway.'

'They'd be worth something if they did,' interjected Calico.

Amy continued, 'It's just been collected together and left here for years, for the use of the Lord Mayors of the City, during their term of office. They have to reside here with their family, for the duration of their term, and treat it like their home. I have heard that the present Lord Mayor lives in a luxuriously furnished flat, so she won't be overly impressed with this. Imagine if you lived in a tiny mid-terrace house, and was elected Lord Mayor and served your term here. You wouldn't want to go home again. It's all free as well, no bills to pay for food and drink, gas and electricity, and so on. And they get a clothing allowance, and visits to the hairdresser paid for; that's a new innovation, seeing as she's the first female mayor. And they get chauffeured everywhere in a Daimler. And they get waited on hand and foot. And they—'

'Okay, I think I've got the picture,' interrupted Calico, 'live the life of Riley.'

'Let's go downstairs and make a pot of tea,' suggested Amy. 'There's not much to do, when the Lord Mayor's out for the afternoon. We get the main of our work done in the morning. Only one of us works in the afternoon, in case she's in for afternoon tea. And one of us works in the evening, that's if there's no functions on. We have to close the bedroom curtains and turn down the bed cover, and make up her hot water bottle and place it in her bed. If they're not going out, you have to draw the parlour room curtains as well, and make them a bedtime drink.' They descended the stairs.

'We aren't into teabags here yet,' said Amy, when they reached the kitchen. 'It has to be special leaf tea. Do you prefer Earl Grey, Assam, Ceylon or Darjeeling?'

'Whatever, it's all the same difference to me. My taste-buds have only sampled supermarket brands,' Calico replied.

'Sometimes I think it's like going back in time, working here. To the old days of servants to the gentry. Everything is done for show. The table-linen is white damask, with an embroidered crest on each item. The napkins; we wash and starch them; have silver, filigree rings to put them in. There's the china: a breakfast service, a dinner service, a tea service, a coffee service, all different; and then the Crown Derby with a crest, for banquets. Five courses, sometimes more, they serve at banquets, and a whole row of knives, forks, and spoons to eat them with. Three different wines, in three different glasses, to accompany the meal, then port, brandy and cigars to finish. It's absolutely amazing how the other half live. All paid for by the ratepayers.' Amy paused for breath.

'That's the second time I've been told that,' retorted Calico, managing to get a word in. 'Who told you before?' demanded Amy.

'The taxi-driver that brought me here,' answered Calico, 'seemed to think he had a say in the running of this place.'

'It's just as well the public doesn't know what goes on here,' replied Amy. 'They might not sit down so contentedly at their two course meal and cup of tea, with their bit of spare cash going on beer and fags, if they saw how much money was squandered here. The Lord Mayor and her guests aren't born to this life though, like titled folk. They act more like the *nouveau riche*, treat it as a novelty, and often over-indulge, put on airs and graces, and show bad manners towards us. Then you have to smile outwardly, and curse them inwardly. It's the only way to get through some of the banquets.'

'You portray a rather ugly picture of these people,' said Calico, disappointed, 'I thought they would be intellectual and sophisticated. The sort my Gran refers to as astocrits.' 'She calls them what?' queried Amy.

'Astocrits. She means aristocrats,' explained Calico, 'Similar to Mrs Malaprop, only she misplaces words, Gran misplaces letters.'

'Oh! Her in Shaw's *The Rivals*. I know who you mean,' interrupted Amy.

'Nearly. It was Sheridan's,' corrected Calico. 'I only knew that because my mother's an actress,' Amy said, ignoring Calico's correction. 'I often help her rehearse. She isn't famous. She does all stage work with travelling repertory companies. Never seems to get the limelight she's always yearned, but she's still optimistic, and thinks one day she'll be noticed.'

'It's a shame,' sympathised Calico, 'You need to appear on television, or in films, before you're recognised as a star nowadays. It's more your marketability than your acting ability.'

Just then a bell sounded. There was a row of bells with the name of a room, and a light, beneath each one, in the hallway. When a bell rang, the light underneath it lit up, so they could see which room they were required to attend. The light was showing beneath the bell for the Mayor's dressing room, which meant Amy was needed to help her off with her outdoor clothes.

Calico, left downstairs by herself, started to wash up the tea things. She was aware of the feeling of being watched. She slowly looked around the big empty kitchen. There, framed in the doorway, was a good-looking man in a smart uniform. He was regarding her with the same look in his eyes, as she had seen in Mr Rolph's that morning; but this time it did not make her feel uncomfortable. Instead, as their eyes met, Calico felt the most odd sensation run through her body. Not unpleasant to her, just not experienced until now. Then he broke the moment with a smile, for as his smile reached his eyes, it obliterated the unnerving look. 'Hello, I'm the Lord Mayor's chauffeur, Charles. No points for guessing that, pretty obvious with this get-up on. You must be the new girl. I've come in for some water to top up the radiator. What's your name?'

'Calico,' she replied, regaining her composure. Although Charles was unaware she had ever lost it. He had given her one of his smouldering, eye-lingering, I-fancy-you stares, and thought she seemed unaffected by it. So, with this observation in mind, he decided to make a quick exit, and not pursue his usual line of chat-up which he felt would not be welcome. All he managed was a lame, 'Goodbye, see you again,' leaving a confused and perplexed Calico, gazing at his retreating back view, troubled by being in close proximity with him for such a short space of time.

The three men Calico had met so far, the taxi-driver, the head butler, the chauffeur, all had provoked a reaction from her. All had changed her preconceived ideas of men in one day. *All men are not like my father and the men I've met back home*, she thought. *These new men are a strange breed, I know nothing about. A whole new experience is waiting. Is this where the threads of Calico begin to intertwine, on that tapestry of life; where many more colours are added to my piece of patchwork?*

Chapter Two

First Sighting

> Beware also of him who flatters you... most probably he has either deceived and abused you, or means to do so.
>
> Sir M. Hale

The next morning Calico was in the kitchen by seven o'clock, as Amy had instructed her, wearing her blue uniform. Already waiting for her was the other parlourmaid. 'I Sophia, you come, Mayor's breakfast.' said this dowdy, dumpy, Italian woman.

'Hello, I'm Calico,' answered Calico politely.

'You come,' repeated Sophia impatiently. 'Lord Mayor's breakfast, now.'

Calico obediently followed her up the stairs, and endeavoured to learn what she was supposed to do, from this unpleasant Italian. She spoke little English, instructing her with hand signals, and sighs and tuts when she got things wrong. Together they arranged the breakfast table with enough accoutrements laid out for ten, not two, people. Calico wondered how she would ever remember all of them, especially with 'Mussolini' hovering menacingly at her elbow, tutting away like a submachine-gun. It was Amy's day off, which meant Sophia would be showing her what to do all morning. Not a pleasant prospect.

As they descended the stairs, the smell of bacon sizzling in hot fat wafted up to greet their nostrils.

'Mmmm, I could fancy a crispy bacon sandwich. The smell gives you an appetite,' said Calico.

Sophia looked at her blankly, '*Ché*?'

'The bacon, smells nice,' repeated Calico.

'*Ché*?' persisted Sophia.

Calico waved her hands at her in a sort of it-doesn't-matter, say-no-more-about-it way. Sophia shrugged her shoulders, frowned, and spouted forth in Italian, waving her hands about to show her displeasure. *If you cut off her hands you would stop her power of speech*, thought Calico. They had reached the kitchen by now.

'Hello,' Cook said, pleasantly. 'You haven't started her off already?' she indicated towards Sophia, who had disappeared into the pantry. 'You wouldn't think she's been over here sixteen years. Never bothered to learn the language. She doesn't have to though, safely cocooned in this place. Can't take to foreigners myself, except for Prince Philip, but then he's almost English now, been here that long. Lovely man, looked after our dear Queen well, kept her happy. I can forgive him for being foreign. I expect the others have told you about me and the Royal Family, love them I do. I suppose it's because I have no family of my own, sort of a substitute. Won't have a word said against them. Listen there's the bell. Take this up to the Mayor and her consort, while it's hot. I don't know what Sophia's doing, absent as usual.'

The first half of the morning passed quickly, with several other members of the household staff coming on duty. Calico met them all at elevenses. For this the cook toasted thick slices of bread; white, brown, and fruit; buttering them while still hot so that they oozed. She piled them high on a plate in the centre of the kitchen table, flanked by a pot of tea and a pot of coffee. Gathered around the table were the cleaners, the parlourmaids, the gardener, sometimes the chauffeur, with the cook seated at the head. The head butler had his tea and toast on a tray in his office. The under-butler resided at the gatehouse, so he had his break with his wife there; but often snitched a couple of pieces of toast to take with him.

Occasionally the housekeeper, Tryphena, appeared. She never sat down to join the others. She took a pot of coffee the cook had ready for her, a plate of toast, and disappeared again. Calico did not know what work the housekeeper did before her break, or after her break, or, come to that, all day. She was too shy to strike up a conversation with Tryphena who had an aura of worldly-wise sophistication surrounding her tall willowy body. With her peaches and cream complexion, blue eyes, and blonde, immaculately cut and styled hair, she made Calico feel awkward in her presence.

A more frequent visitor at breaktime was Mr· Rolph's son. He worked for a local laundry, and of course the firm had the contract for all the Mansion House laundry. If he was in the area, even if it was not his delivery day there, he would call in for tea and toast, and to see his wife, who was employed as a cleaner.

The talk around the table was interesting to Calico. The lives of these people were far removed from the quiet, safe, lives of the people she had met thus far in her life. She learned through the course of their conversation, that Grace, one of the cleaners; a large blousey woman, with bleached blonde hair, and smudged scarlet lipstick; had seven children. Her eldest daughter had an illegitimate child. Her husband drank to excess, and she often came in with a black eye, as a result. Susan, another cleaner, was having trouble with a straying husband. She was tall and slender, with long blonde hair and pale blue eyes. She wore long flowing skirts and cheesecloth tops, and went barefoot.

Maria, also a cleaner, was the head butler's daughter-in-law, and very friendly with Sophia as a fellow Italian, and also because she was a parlourmaid with her, before her marriage. Apparently she was having trouble starting a family, and was undergoing all sorts of tests to sort it out. The other cleaner was Vera, she was a quiet, staid, sensible spinster, who looked after her aged mother. She had her hair cut very short, and wore trousers all the time, which Mr Rolph did not approve of at all.

'See you walked into another door last night, Grace,' remarked Susan. 'That's a beaut of a shiner you've got there.'

'Shows he comes home at night,' retorted Grace.

'Yes, you can't say your husband doesn't give you any attention. I don't know which of us is worse off,' answered Susan.

'It's only his way,' said Grace, giving the same answer to excuse her husband she had been using for years.

'Is there any greater torment than love?' murmured Vera. The others looked at her with astonishment. It was an unusual statement for a spinster, but they all let it pass unremarked upon.

'Time's up,' stated Olive. The timing of breaks was her responsibility, and if she said the time was up, there was no arguing. A shuffling of feet and scraping of chairs met this remark. Everyone went back to their posts. Calico to cleaning the consort's dressing room. She heard the Mayor return. Before she could vacate the room, the consort entered. 'Hello, Missy,' he said.

He called all young ladies, Missy, because he had such a bad memory for names.

'Oh dear! I seem to have picked up a few hairs on my suit. I wonder if you would be kind enough to brush them off for me,' he asked, pointing to the clothes brush on his dressing table. Calico could not see any hairs on his suit.

'Sorry, whereabouts did you say they were?'

'You may as well brush it all over. Brush firmly, be sure to get them then,' he answered. Calico brushed as firmly as she could.

'Brush harder, Missy. Hairs seem to stick stubbornly to this type of cloth.'

Calico brushed as hard as she could, expecting him to rebuke her for treating his suit so roughly.

'Lewis, are you ready? It's nearly time we left for the luncheon buffet at the Council House,' called out the Lord Mayor. I'm on my way downstairs. I thought we would have an aperitif before we leave. Do hurry up.'

'Coming dear,' the consort replied obediently. 'Thank you, that will do,' he said to Calico. 'Here,' and he pushed a five pound note into her hand. Calico was taken by surprise.

'No, sir. I could not take it. I'm only doing my job.' Calico gave it back to him. 'You are paid to look after the Lord Mayor, not me,' he retorted.

'I'd rather not take it. Thank you, sir.' Calico made a quick exit, before the consort had a chance to press her with the money again. Calico could not justify receiving five pounds for brushing down his suit. It did not seem quite right, being given all that money, for brushing a few hairs off a suit.

Calico stayed behind the door of the backstairs, out of sight, until she heard the consort come out of his room and proceed down the main staircase. She opened the door to return to the consort's dressing room, to finish her cleaning, and came face to face with the chauffeur, who was coming out of the Mayor's dressing room. Her heart did something, she did not know what. This time it was not pleasant, it was a sharp pain, and then she could feel it beating: similar to the time she had been given a double dose of the injection at the dentists. There was an attraction about him; was it the intense emotion he put into his dark brown eyes, when he looked at her. Was it the loose-limbed movement of his lithe body? Was it the caress he used in his voice? It was the most odd occurrence, how her body reacted to him without her approval.

'Hello, again. I've brought up the old dear's shopping for her. More hats, she looks a sight in all of them. She would look better in a bee-keeper's get-up,' he said cheekily. Calico knew he said something, because she seen his lips move, but she did not really hear any of it. She smiled stupidly at him, quickly went into the consort's room, and closed the door behind her. He thought she had smiled sarcastically at him, and went on his way thinking how unfriendly this new girl seemed.

Calico zoomed round the room, to finish the cleaning at top speed, and to stop thoughts of a certain man invading her head. She went downstairs to join the others for lunch. The table was already laid; so she helped carry the hot plates and the full serving dishes, through to the staff dining room.

The cleaners went home at lunchtime, but they were all fed before they left. Such is the generosity of employers, who are not using money from their own pockets, and do not have to worry about profit and loss, trading accounts and balance sheets, and have no fear of going bankrupt. Such coffers are always replenished by the general public, unknowingly bearing the burden of financing these little extras, by contributing their rates without question, because it is the law. 'I'm not really hungry, but I suppose I'd better eat something. Pass me the carrots please Vera,' said Susan, apathetically.

'In Italia, war, no pasti,' recounted Sophia. 'Molto hungry, soldato fire houses, steala food, cattivo, cattivo soffrire. We life hand-mouth.' This was said with plenty of hand movement to emphasise her words.

'How awful,' sympathised Calico, understanding her. 'No food, German soldiers treating you so badly.'

'No German,' interrupted Sophia. 'English.'

'Oh! That's all right then,' replied Calico. The others, excepting Maria, exchanged amused glances.

Vera quickly changed the subject, fearing a confrontation between Calico and the two Italians. She hated arguments, even when they did not directly involve herself. 'What are you doing this afternoon,' she enquired of Calico.

'I'm going for a walk on the Downs, after I've washed, starched and ironed my apron, ready for this evening.'

Calico enjoyed her walk. She liked looking at all the buildings, each with a character all its own, imagining how it used to be, in this old part of the city, at the time that authors like Dickens and Ainsworth were writing their novels. These palatial mansions were four or five storeys high, surrounded by extensive gardens. They were built here by influential rich merchants, well away from the sordid hovels surrounding the sea port, through which their main source of income was obtained. No hustle and bustle, or beggars in rags, intruded their peaceful seclusion. Calico thought that the world had not changed so much, since those times. The wealthy still encompassed themselves with materialistic symbols of opulence: while their workers lived in tightly packed terraced houses, or sky high blocks of flats.

Being a country lass, the worst thing imaginable for Calico would be to live where there was no space to yourself; having to step out of your front door straight into the street, or a corridor. But then Calico was a loner. She had not yet learnt to thrive in the company of other people, and gain a stimulus from being with them. Perhaps she never would, some need the company of people to survive and some do not.

Calico was taking the path through a churchyard, reading the gravestones, when Amy caught up with her.

'Hi, Calico,' said Amy a little breathlessly.

'Hello, Amy,' greeted Calico, surprised to see her. 'What have you been doing today?'

'I've been into the shopping centre. Bought a new dress for this evening,' answered Amy. 'I've come back to change, before I go out. You live quite near where that pop festival's being held don't you?'

'Yes, not far. Why are you going?'

'Like to; have to do a bit of swapping of shifts, and brown-nosing to Soppy and Rolphie to get enough time off. Will you be going, or will you swap your weekend off with me? It would make life easier for me.' said Amy, hopefully.

'Sorry,' apologised Calico. 'I'm going to the festival. You can stay at my place, if you get Sophia to swap, unless you have other plans. You're quite welcome.'

'That would be great,' enthused Amy. 'We could go together. I was going on my own, but I would rather have company.'

By this time they had reached their rooms at the top of the Mansion House. Amy had an electric kettle in her room, and invited Calico in for coffee.

Several weeks after this, Calico was again in Amy's room having coffee, and talking about the pop festival.

'I can't decide what to wear,' Amy said, looking at Calico, then she frowned. 'Your hair looks severe tied back like that. Why don't you put it up for evening duty?'

'I've never tried to put it up, I don't really know how to do it. I suppose that's why I've never bothered,' admitted Calico.

'I'll do it for you, and make up your face,' offered Amy. 'If we're going to the pop festival together, we'll have to pull out all the stops to get a couple of blokes, with all that extra competition around.'

Calico was not sure she wanted to get a bloke, at the festival, but she went along with Amy, allowing her to fix her hair and make up her face, without protesting.

Back in her own room, Calico changed into her evening uniform. She glanced in the mirror, she knew it was her face looking back at her, but it was not the face she was familiar with, not the face she had grown up with. This was not the face of a girl, this was the face of a young woman. Could she face the world looking so different, wearing this façade? She felt a charlatan. Her mirror image looked experienced and sophisticated. The eyes, seemed to hold a secret knowledge. Well, there was no time to change it, she had to report for duty in five minutes. She went downstairs. As she arrived in the hallway, a bell sounded. It was from the Mayor's dressing room. Calico hurried upstairs to see what she wanted.

'Help me with this hat. Sophia helped me dress, but now I've decided to change hats. Put the pin through the back, there by my finger,' ordered the Lord Mayor.

No please or thank you Calico noted, doing as she was bid.

'Here, take my coat and take it down to the chauffeur. Ask him to put it in the back of the car; I may need it later. You can go out through the front entrance,' she said, handing over her expensive fur to Calico.

Calico went downstairs and out of the front door. The chauffeur was standing by the driver's door of the Daimler. He did not recognise Calico immediately. She stood before him, holding out the coat, her eyes met his. She was sure his eyes opened wider, and they looked almost black the pupil had spread so much. She heard his sharp intake of breath, and waited for him to say something, as his mouth was open ready. Nothing was forthcoming. Then Calico ended their mutual admiration by informing him that the Lord Mayor wanted her coat placed in the back of the car. Calico realised something strange had happened. For the moment there was no chatty conversation from Charles, he had gone silent. He took the fur from her, putting it into the back of the car as instructed.

Calico took this opportunity to make her getaway. She hurried to the side entrance, entered the kitchen, and sat down feeling weak. She also felt nauseous when her nose came in contact with the lingering odour of what Sophia had cooked for her tea, the remains of which, were in a pan on the stove. Red and green peppers simmered in olive oil and garlic. Calico decided beans on toast, with a layer of melted cheese and a fried egg on top, would be easiest and quickest for her own meal. She could hear the television, so she assumed Sophia was watching it in the staff sitting room.

Calico ate her meal, washed up, went over to the fruit bowl and selected a large juicy pear. She had only taken one bite, when she heard foot-falls in the corridor, and Charles appeared at the door. Her body tensed. Charles approached her. He had regained his self-confidence. Earlier, when Calico had appeared with the coat, he had been stunned. He had thought her attractive before, but with the make-up enhancing her best features, a transformation had taken place. She was very good-looking and seductive. Her sexy come-to-bed eyes, under long lashes; her full lips glistening and moist, made him ache to hold her, look deep into her eyes, and cover her lips with his. He wanted her to groan with pleasure, he wanted her to respond with the same intensity of feeling. That was why he had just turned away, and remained silent. He knew he could not rush her, that he could not suddenly crush her to him in a passionate embrace, and kiss her until they had no breath left in their bodies. He was relieved she had made a quick exit. It gave him time to get over that sudden rush of blood to his head; that momentary madness, when outside uncontrollable influences collide with powerful passions. He knew he would return to see her, after dropping off the Mayor. It was unavoidable. She had churned up so much feeling inside of him that he had to see her. He also knew it was unwise to do so, not because he was a married man; but because he wanted her too much. He had not felt this way for years. He did not believe in love at first sight. Surely, if there was such a thing, with all the women he had known, it would have happened to him by now.

'You don't usually come back here. Have you forgotten something?' said Calico, quite aware of the reason he had returned so quickly.

His words were charged with meaning, 'I haven't forgotten anything,' he said, meeting Calico's eyes and holding them with his own. 'That's why I came back. I wanted another look at that beautiful face of yours. You look stunning tonight. Mmm, that pear looks ripe, give us a bite.'

Calico handed it over in a bemused state, and watched while he bit sensuously into the creamy-white flesh. Licking the juice slowly from around the corners of his mouth, all the while keeping his eyes on her. Calico felt uneasy, observing the long pink tongue playing around the lips, languorously licking, then darting in and out between even white teeth; but she was transfixed by the display. Charles was accomplished at this: he could use his eyes, mouth, tongue, hands, his whole body, to convey sexual connotations.

Charles moved nearer to her, intending to put the pear to her mouth. Calico intervened with her hand, and took the pear from him, before it reached her lips. In so doing their hands touched. Calico had been out with several boys back home, even kissed a few, but nothing had felt like this.

This was crazy. A person's presence, a slight brush of skin against skin, caused the most untold disruption inside her. He moved closer. She thought he was going to kiss her. He thought he was going to kiss her. 'Why here?' demanded the looming shape of Sophia. 'Why no 'ome wid Signora Charles e bambino. Why here?'

They both took a step back, both faces coloured, as if they had been caught in a compromising position. Calico felt as if Sophia had struck her physically, the crushing blow she felt from those few words. She never considered the possibility of him being married. *At least*, she thought, *Charles has the decency to look embarrassed*. Charles's high colour was not attributable to embarrassment, but annoyance. He preferred to get a woman totally under his spell, before he mentioned the wife and kids. Often he only made the admission when he wanted to end a relationship that he thought had run its course. Besides this time it was different. He desperately wanted to be with Calico. He could not, now, get her image out of his mind. He was hooked, well and truly. For the first time in his life, he was suffering the agonies that he had put numerous women through, with his thoughtless behaviour.

'Signora visit mother,' Charles finally answered. 'Me wait here until fetch Mayor.' It was difficult not to lapse into stilted English, when talking to Sophia, it was all she understood.

'Si, si, you go now,' ordered Sophia.

'No. I stay here,' replied Charles, defiantly. Sophia did one of her usual shoulder shrugs, accompanied by a series of tuts, and retreated to the staff sitting room.

Charles was aware it would take a long time to regain the position he had just lost. It would take all his wiles, all his powers of persuasion, to become as close to Calico again. He could not give her up. His head said, *Stop this now nothing has happened.* His heart and body said, *I can't, I want her.*

It is difficult to do the honourable thing and turn away in these circumstances. Life is so short, so full of tragedy, that when an opportunity, however brief, of complete and utter happiness presents itself, the immediate reaction is to snatch at it greedily. But then the sensible among us stop and think, consider others and make up a whole list of reasons for not going through with it, and then regret it for the rest of our lives. Not Charles, he had no such problem. Live for the moment, was his selfish attitude to life, and damn everybody else.

Calico stated the obvious. 'You're married, Charles. I should have realised.'

'I thought you knew,' he lied. 'Everyone else in the Mansion House does, I assumed you did too.'

'With children,' Calico continued as if he had not spoken.

Charles did not answer. The less she persisted with this conversation the better. He did not want to talk about his wife and kids with her, they were a separate part of his life.

Calico went over to the radio and turned it on, as if a stranger talking would blot out her own thoughts. It was Country and Western music. She turned it up quite loud, and sat listening to the songs. Charles could not talk over the music without shouting. What he wanted to say needed to be said in a low intimate voice, so he stayed quiet.

They sat in silence. Each very much aware of the others presence, the atmosphere heavy with unspoken words and both were thinking of the other, neither knowing what to do. Calico went over to the radio. Watching her movements, Charles could stand it no longer, his emotions overcame him. He rose from his chair and stood behind Calico, turning her round to face him. He kissed her with all the passion that had been welling up inside of him.

'Oh Calico,' he murmured, his voice half-strangled with emotion, 'I want you so much.' Then he turned on his heel and walked out.

Chapter Three

In the Butler's Bad Books

If punishment makes not the will supple, it hardens the offender.

Locke

One morning, about a week after the incident with the chauffeur, Calico was summoned to report to the head butler in his office. She found Mr Rolph sat behind his desk, wearing quite different clothes than usual. Calico noticed the tights and buckle shoes, she smiled, about to make a comment, but meeting the stern face before her, she thought better of it. Mr Rolph admonished her for playing loud pop music, and chatting to the chauffeur, while on duty. 'The kitchen is not to be used as a social club. When on duty you should behave in a proper manner. You are representing the Mansion House, and I expect you to conduct yourself with propriety,' he scolded her.

'It was not pop music, it was country and western, and I didn't ask the chauffeur into the kitchen,' replied Calico, indignantly.

'I have it on good authority that I am right on both accounts. We will say no more about it,' Mr Rolph said, getting up from his desk and putting his arm around Calico's shoulders. 'You will not let it happen again, will you? Or I shall have to reconsider your appointment. If you will be guided by me, you could do yourself a lot of good. I look favourably on people who try to please me, but I make an unpleasant adversary.' He smiled kindly at Calico. She considered the smile to be halfway between a sneer and a leer, and wondered what was inferred by his last statement. The best thing to do, she decided, was to ignore it, in case he enlightened her. To get the interview over as quickly as possible, Calico dropped her defence and replied meekly, 'Yes Mr Rolph.'

'I think we understand each other,' said Mr Rolph, giving her a level gaze. Then he caught hold of her hand and kissed it. 'You may go now, but bear in mind my words, my dear.' Calico made her way towards the kitchen.

This was only the second time Calico had been alone with Mr Rolph, and she felt uneasy about him each time. The look on his face sent a wave of revulsion through her body. When he touched her she had to steel herself against the impulse to shrink away from him.

Calico had never paid much attention to her body before, it was just there. She fed it fuel, and it performed to her will. But now it had developed a life of its own; she did not seem able to control its reactions towards people. She was aware of things inside of her, other than an efficient digestive system. Odd feelings surging through her that she found difficult to understand. Was this agony part of growing up? she wondered. Did it get easier as you grew older? Did you manage to control these feelings through experience? She hoped so. She did not like what was happening to her. She had always believed in God: was this the temptation the Bible warned to fight against? The sins of the flesh, fight against your own body. Was life then to be a perpetual battle?

'Calico, you're not listening to me,' rebuked Amy, who had met Calico in the hallway. 'I asked you a question. What did Rolphie want to see you about?'

Calico, brought out of her thoughts, apologised, 'Sorry, Amy. That sneak Sophia reported me to Mr Rolph. Told him I was playing loud pop music, and entertaining the chauffeur.'

'And were you?' questioned Amy.

'Not exactly. It was country and western music, and the chauffeur only stayed a short while. Sophia was there most of the time,' explained Calico. 'She exaggerated it.'

'Bitch. We ought to get even with her. I'll think up something,' retorted Amy vehemently. 'She's always telling tales to Rolphie, but then you couldn't get much closer to his ear than she does.'

Calico was going to ask Amy to elaborate on that remark, but as they entered the kitchen, there seemed to be a lot of excitement going on, and she let it pass for the moment.

'Quick, come on you two,' said the cook, with an air of urgency, 'or you'll miss it!' They followed her and the others outside.

The scene that awaited them was like a picture, taken from the pages of a history book. In the courtyard at the front of the house, was the old coach and horses belonging to the city. These were brought out on special occasions. Apparently this special occasion was the collection of the Dignitaries, of the city in France that Brydle was twinned with, from the local airport. Then taking them on a tour of the City.

All the entourage was decked out in their livery. The head butler and the under-butler were attired in crimson coats decorated with gold braid; crimson plush knee breeches; pink silk stockings and buckled shoes. They were acting as footmen for the spectacle. The coach driver, the chauffeur and the Lord Mayor's secretary, were dressed in black and gold braid, white breeches and stockings. They fronted the coach. All five wore embroidered tunics under their coats, and hats with plumes.

The Lord Mayor wore a scarlet cloak with white ermine trim and her heavy gold chain of office. Her usual awful choice of headwear had been replaced by a tricorn hat. The consort looked drab and out of place, like a hornet at a butterfly ball.

Calico took in the whole scene: the vibrant colours; the fairytale coach; with its gold coat of arms emblazoned on the side; the Lord Mayor looking more like a wicked witch, with her thin lips and hooked nose, than a fairy queen; but nevertheless beautifully attired. The matching pair of chestnut bays and dapple greys, their muscles taut, straining, were ready to be off at the first light touch on the reins. Her eyes rested on Charles, looking more heart-breaking than ever. The black of coat and hat bringing out his dark good looks. Sensing this, he turned his head and winked at her. She averted her gaze quickly, sure that her face was mirroring the colour of the footmen's jackets. A couple of policemen on motorbikes appeared through the wrought iron gates, which rather spoilt the pageant as they led off the procession.

The residue of the staff trooped back into the Mansion House. There began a fervour of activity, in anticipation of the foreign visitors. The finishing touches were added to the guest suite, and the dining room. Cook was busy preparing the food for the banquet that evening, to which all the local dignitaries, and a Lord and Lady or two, had been invited.

Amy had hatched a plot to get Sophia into trouble. She told Calico about it that morning. This being the first time there had been a female Mayor, Sophia was quick to see her chance. She had tried to make herself more of a lady's
than a parlourmaid by offering to do her washing, ir
and sewing and generally fawning and trying to in

herself with the Lord Mayor, thinking that it would be easier work and a better position. Amy knew it would do no good to try and get Sophia into trouble with Mr Rolph, as he would cover up for her and it would go no further, so it had to be something that would get her into trouble with the Mayor. What they would do Amy decided, was starch a couple of items of the Mayor's undergarments. Amy was on duty that afternoon, so she would select the items from Sophia's freshly washed and ironed pile, soak them in starch at the same time as she did her apron, and put them on the dryer hidden with her apron. Then somehow, during the course of the evening, they would secrete them back into the pile of laundry that Sophia would take upstairs, and place in the Lord Mayor's dressing room.

'As we are not on duty tomorrow, and leaving late tonight to go to the pop festival, no one can prove it was us,' finished Amy conspiratorially.

'Nice one,' enthused Calico.

Some of the lads in Calico's village had agreed to collect her and Amy that evening. A gang of them sometimes came up to go to clubs in the city. There was not much excitement for them in the village, and often not even in the surrounding towns. It was more expensive for entrance fees and drinks in the city, and there was the extra petrol needed, so they made the trip when they had got enough money together. Calico hoped the village lads would not be too rowdy and boisterous after their drinking session, but then they were used to rough cider, so beer should not affect them unduly. She did not think they would create a good impression on the posh folk attending the feast that night so she had asked them to wait out of sight, until the guests had gone, to avoid any aggravation.

Calico spent her afternoon sewing patchwork inserts into her faded straight-leg jeans. These she had possessed for several years, but since the fashion now was for flared trousers, she thought she would economise by making her old jeans into flared ones for the pop festival the next day. When she had finished them, she laid out on the bed the clothes she would travel home in, packed a few things in her overnight bag, and left everything ready to grab quickly, as soon as Mr Rolph said she could go. Then she changed into her evening uniform, put her hair up, lightly made up her face, and went downstairs to join the other staff.

With the exception of the housekeeper and the gardener, everybody was on duty. Even the cleaners had been brought in to help with the washing-up. The staff dining-table had been extended to its limit, to enable them all to be seated at it for their evening meal. To make it easier for the cook, the meal was ham salad with chunks of crusty bread, fruit with cream, and cheese and biscuits.

To help serve the food and drink at the banquet, temporary waitresses from an agency had been employed. They seemed to do very well out of Mr Rolph. They were fed on arrival, supplied with drinks throughout the evening, and given some of the leftovers to take home with them, much to the disapproval of the permanent staff.

The cook as usual had everything under control. She worried all week, panicked all day, until she knew everything was ready; then sat down half an hour before serving time, with a sigh of relief and a teacupful of sherry. Then she mentally went through the menu, checking the dishes off in her head to make sure she had not forgotten anything. Calico appeared just at this moment, so she was roped in to help, as a second pair of eyes. 'Turtle soup ready, needs cream adding last minute before putting into tureens, keeping warm in hot-cupboard. Lemon sole in bain-marie. Garnishes: chopped parsley, croûtons, lemon twirls, tomato rosettes, and single cream; all prepared.'

'Yes,' agreed Calico. 'All here.'

'Ducks portioned, balls of sage and onion stuffing, apple sauce made. Serving dishes decorated with piped mashed potato and browned. Roast potatoes in oven, new potatoes simmering on stove. Carrots' water on and salted, peas same. Gravy made. Meat plates, gravy boats, veg. dishes, in hot-cupboard. Dessert prepared.'

The cook's knowledge of her trade was limited, which accounted for the fact that every banquet menu was virtually the same. The turtle soup was out of tins. The dessert was always slices of fresh pineapple, put on individual plates, with fresh strawberries, raspberries, loganberries, chopped peaches, sliced kiwi fruit, and peeled grapes, piled up in the centre. Lashings of clotted cream accompanied this dish, served in separate silver jugs. Whether the fruits were in season or not was no problem. Mr Rolph would obtain them, damn the expense, from somewhere. (Just as he always got Sophia's truffles.) 'Cheese and biscuits, already upstairs. I'm ready for the fray,' announced cook.

'Right, ladies, to your posts. At the double, quick march,' commanded Mr Rolph's booming voice from the hallway. Figures scattered hither and thither in nothing remotely akin to an orderly fashion, but as everyone knew where they were going, it did not matter. Mr Rolph would have liked to drill them like a regiment as it would have given him great pleasure to see them march in single file, instead of in gaggles of two or three, gossiping and giggling along the way.

Mr Rolph loved women (or rather he loved the pleasure they gave him), but he had no respect for them. He thought them silly, shallow, selfish creatures (a clear case of the pot calling the kettle black) but then he never actually got into deep conversation with them. He never got to know them mentally, only physically, he knew only their surface value, and did not bother to discover what lay beneath. Mr Rolph would go on believing, until the day he died, that man was the superior race. Women were put on Earth for his benefit, to see to his comforts and his pleasures; not as an equal partner, but as an accessory.

Calico went upstairs to the entrance hall. The under-butler opened the front door for the guests and ushered them into the hall where they were relieved of their coats and hats, by two parlourmaids. These were then taken upstairs, and hung up in the spare dressing room. The head butler and the other parlourmaid served aperitifs to the guests who congregated in the Lord Mayor's parlour.

Calico managed to have a quick word with Amy, in between ferrying the guests' outer clothing about. She discovered Amy had carried out the first part of the plan. The Lord Mayor's long line bra and matching pants were stiff as a board, and could stand up on their own. This knowledge made it difficult for them to keep a straight face that evening, when the Mayor made her entrance.

She reminded Calico of the lines of a song: 'Stately as a galleon, she sailed across the floor.' Her huge bust stuck out about the same amount as her bottom, so that her figure resembled an elongated S, when viewed from the side. Her dresses, always of good quality, were never cut to disguise her figure, rather they seemed to accentuate it, clinging in all the wrong places. The consort, resembling a black-winged bumble bee in his evening dress, followed closely behind his wife. He stopped to have a word with Amy, whereupon a sharp whistle from the Lord Mayor, quickly brought him back to her heel. They both disappeared into the parlour to socialise. Calico and Amy went into the middle room, where the food and drink were stationed.

There were fifty people attending dinner, covered by five waitresses, three parlourmaids, two wine waiters (well one was the under-butler and the other was a waitress), and Mr Rolph to supervise the proceedings.

Calico thought he spent most of his time touching the waitresses at every opportunity, when he thought no one was observing him. *Is that what he meant by 'looking favourably on people who try to please me'?* Calico wondered. The waitresses did play up to him, and did not seem to mind what he was doing.

The diners had now reached the cheese and biscuit course. Calico was amazed they still had room left in their stomachs for more food. All the silver serving dishes had been brought back empty, re-filled, and returned empty again. The cream was requested as if there was a Jersey cow or two on tap.

It made Calico feel guilty: all this gluttony and indulgence when there were so many families struggling on low incomes in her village. Even serving the food made her feel an accomplice, as if by so doing she was in agreement with it. She had that hopeless feeling of knowing that no action of hers would change this situation. She could go into the dining room, make known her point of view in front of all these influential people, and resign from her post in protest, but what good would that do? Would it put more money into the hands of the needy? No it would not change a thing. She remembered what Amy had said, 'Smile outwardly, curse inwardly.' Calico now realised what she meant by that remark. What else was there to do? So, smiling outwardly she cleared away the rest of the cutlery and china from the dining table, and handed round the cigars and cigarettes. Amy followed in her wake with the lighter. The under-butler preceded them with the port and brandy. Sophia re-filled the chocolate mints and sugared almond dishes.

At this juncture the females were segregated to the parlour, and the males were left to tell dirty stories, swear, curse, and follow other manly pursuits.

After a time, when the men thought the ladies must be missing their company, they favoured them with their presence in the drawing room, and kept the staff busy serving spirits to them. Calico was tempted to take the bottle in for one red-cheeked chap for no sooner had she served him his drink, and then served somebody else, he was ready for another. 'Make it a treble, my dear girl. It'll save you a trip,' he slurred at her. She later found out he was one of the Lords. So she was relieved she had not had the temerity to offer him the bottle.

When the kitchen staff had left and the under-butler had gone over to the gatehouse, Mr Rolph went downstairs with the waitresses. He doled out the food he had kept back for them, and a bottle of wine each. He received a kiss and a cuddle from each of them in payment. He returned upstairs well-pleased, making sure to lock the door to the downstairs, so that no one else could take the food and wine he had saved himself. He told Amy and Calico to finish clearing up the middle room, and instructed Sophia to help him with the guests' coats. Because the guests often gave tips when they had enjoyed their evening, he made sure he and Sophia were the only beneficiaries of these.

Calico and Amy were tidying up as they had been bid, when Amy suddenly exclaimed, 'I've got it!' Before Calico could make a remark Amy continued, 'If we take the shelf out of the dumb waiter, I could just about squeeze into it. You press the down button and send me kitchenwards. When I've put the starched underwear in with the Lord Mayor's other things, and I'm ready to come back up, I'll hammer on the side of the lift, and you press the up button. Old Rolphie will have locked the door at the top of the first flight of stairs by now. He thinks no one knows he does that, because we usually go straight upstairs, after a late night do. I bet he allows us to leave by the main entrance tonight, and sees us out, which will give us a cast-iron alibi, when he tries to blame us for the Lord Mayor's discomfort. Okay, going down. Ground floor, ladies' fashions; basement, starched undies...'

Calico hoped nobody would come through the door. She crossed her fingers, and everything she had two of, and stayed nervously by the lift waiting. The door knob turned. Calico froze. The door opened. Calico unfroze and pretended to be sorting out the cutlery. It was Mr Rolph. 'Have you not finished in here, yet?' he asked, impatiently.

'Not quite,' answered Calico, 'nearly done.' This was awful. She tensed, waiting for the obvious remark.

'Where is Amy?' he questioned.

'She's in the dining room, making sure all the things for washing-up have been collected,' lied Calico, willing him to go away.

Mr Rolph had no reason to doubt her words. He knew Amy could not have gone downstairs as it was locked, and she could not have gone upstairs or he would have seen her.

'I will go and hurry her up,' he said, his hand on the dining room door knob. *Oh no!* Calico's mind screamed, *This is trouble.*

'Mr Rolph,' boomed the Mayor's far from dulcet tones. He removed his hand from the door knob. Calico breathed an audible sigh of relief, and disguised it as a cough.

'Tell Amy to hurry up, would you?' he asked.

'Yes, I will,' replied Calico, moving towards the dining room door.

'That is the trouble with letting a woman be Lord Mayor, they are much more demanding than men,' grumbled Mr Rolph, as he made his exit to find out what the Mayor wanted him to do.

No sooner had the door closed behind him, than there were banging noises coming from the dumb waiter. Calico pressed the up button. 'The deed is done,' announced Amy.

'Here take this, while I climb out of here. There isn't much room in one of these. I caught my bum on the way down, it must stick out more than I thought. Careful with that bag.'
'What's in here?' asked Calico, surveying the plastic carrier Amy had passed to her.

'It's quite heavy. Not the silver,' she joked. 'The greedy old goat had stashed a load of food and drink downstairs. So I helped myself to a couple of bottles of wine, some cold roast potatoes, bread rolls, duck portions, cheese, and sugared almonds. That should see us through tomorrow at the pop festival. I've put my starched apron covering the top. Now all I've got to do, is get it upstairs; without Laurel and Hardy and the two ugly sisters spotting it. You go into the hall and see if anybody's about. If it's all clear, come back and tell me. If not, pretend you went in to the hall to ask Mr Rolph if we can go now.'

'You do take risks, Amy,' laughed Calico.

'So what, they aren't life and death ones, are they? Serve the old sod right. If I'd taken the lot, it would have been the first time he went home empty-handed,' retorted Amy. 'Now go on, quick.'

Calico checked the hall; it was empty. She could hear raised voices coming from outside. 'I fought for you in the war, my lad. So show some respect.' That was Mr Rolph's voice. The lads from the village must have arrived. Still, never mind, the diversion would allow Amy to get her plunder upstairs without interference. Calico opened the door. 'All clear Amy,' she whispered.

They went up the stairs together. 'The lads from the village are here. Mr Rolph is arguing with them on the front doorstep.'

'Has he mentioned the war yet?' asked Amy.

'Of course,' answered Calico. They laughed.

Calico changed, picked up her overnight bag, and went to fetch Amy. She knocked on Amy's door, and entered.

Amy had changed into a low-cut, bright pink T-shirt, and a pair of purple velvet flared trousers. The top half of which followed the contours of her body like a second skin.

'I didn't realise you had such a large bust,' said Calico, amazed at Amy's cleavage.

'Well you wouldn't. I haven't any reason to flaunt it here, so I keep it covered up,' answered Amy, matter-of-factly.

Over the T-shirt and trousers, Amy put on a black leather jacket with fringes. She had reddish-brown hair, green eyes, a long sharp nose, and an over-sized mouth. She was not good-looking, but she had a stunning figure coupled with an attractive personality.

As they made their way downstairs, they could hear snatches of the conversation still going on, between Mr Rolph and the village boys. 'If you had been in the war, and seen your comrades killed, cut down in the prime of life by the grim reaper—'

'That's old Farmer Tuscott at harvest time, when he has to pay us overtime to get it all in afore it rains. He's a grim reaper then,' interrupted one of the lads.

'You would be ashamed to wear that around your neck then,' continued Mr Rolph, ignoring the interruption. 'It is an insult to all British servicemen.'

A couple of the lads were into motorbikes and Hell's Angels. One of them had found an iron cross and wore it for decoration. This is what, understandably, incensed the older man. To the youngsters it had meant nothing, except they knew it had something to do with the Nazis. Now it meant a reaction from the stuffy older generation; another way they could irritate them, besides revving up their bikes, playing loud music, letting their hair grow long, and wearing tattered unwashed jeans.

As Calico and Amy appeared Mr Rolph turned his attention to them. 'I do not know how nice girls like you could associate with these lads. What a low-life element of society they are. Queen and country mean nothing to them. A few years in the services would soon sort them out. Discipline is needed to make a fine upstanding fellow.'

'A couple of beers does that to mine,' remarked a lad, laughing at his own joke.

'Pompous ass,' murmured Amy to Calico.

'What did you say?' demanded Mr Rolph.

'It's in the past,' said Calico quickly covering for her.

'Not for me, and many like me. We relive every day the horror of the tormented cries of the wounded, the awful conditions we survived. It is always with us, haunting us, we cannot put it in our past. Then you see youngsters with their attitude. We were fighting for the freedom of the following generation at their age, for their freedom. And are they grateful? Not a bit; what a waste, they could not give a damn that some of us gave our lives,' concluded Mr Rolph.

One of the lads addressed Calico. 'Do we have to wait for the Last Post or can we go now?'

Mr Rolph stood glowering over the party for a minute or two, looking as though he was going to say something more. Deciding he was wasting his breath on them, he went inside, slamming the door behind him.

'Phew!' said a lad. 'Do you get a lecture like that every day?'

'No,' answered Amy. 'We do all we can to keep him off the subject of his wartime activities. Old hypocrite, talking about fine upstanding fellows. He may have been once, but he isn't any more. There's a lot of stories I could tell about him, and his holier-than-thou attitude, that would put dents in the halo he carries around with him.'

Chapter Four

The Pop Festival

Our advantages fly away;
Gather flowers while ye may.

Ovid

'The cock's crowing, his harem's fed,
Phoebie's risen above the cow shed,
The dawn chorus has now bin said,
And you two buggers be still a-bed,' shouted Calico's father up the stairs. 'Thought thee wanted to git up 'arly. I woke thee afore I got the beasts in, and thee still bisn't up.'

'Okay, I'm awake now. Thank you,' re-iterated Calico. 'Excuse the rude awakening,' she shouted to Amy in the next room. 'Remember we've got a guest, Dad.'

'We don't 'ave guests 'ere, we d'ave friends; guests is fer 'otels an' sich like,' he answered her.

'Yes, Dad.'

Calico found it difficult to get the better of her father, he always had an answer ready. They argued often, but it was always good-naturedly. This latter quality extended into his way of life. He took everything in his stride; you could not hurry him, and you could not worry him. He went along at the same steady pace day after day, whatever disaster befell him. 'Here we suffer grief and pain, over the road it's just the same,' he would say, realising he was not singled out by

God, it was nothing personal. Everyone had their share of suffering. It was no good dwelling on it, you had to put it behind you and carry on with life.

Calico put on the now flared jeans with the patchwork inserts, a long turquoise T-shirt, and a purple leather waistcoat with two-foot-long fringes hanging from the waist, and went downstairs.

Her father and mother were in the kitchen having their ritual: early morning tea and biscuits before milking; they breakfasted later. Her father was dunking his biscuits in his tea and as usual one fell in; he was fishing about for it with his spoon when Calico appeared. 'I thought you would've got the hang of biscuit dunking by now. You've been practising for so many years, you should have it off to a tee,' Calico teased him.

He smiled, deepening the lines of his weathered skin, around the outer corners of his pale blue-grey eyes, and showing the few teeth he still had left. He had never been to a dentist in his life, and no amount of pressurising, persuading, or cajoling by Calico and his wife, could get him there.

He countered Calico's remark with, 'Thee's got 'n 'ole in thee pants, best let Mother put a patch on it afore thee goes out.'

'It's supposed to be there. It's wear. You have to keep them original,' she retorted.

'Oh! 'Tis the fashion I s'pose to 'ave 'oles in thee pants. Just think o' that Mother. Ole Ted an' ole Joe bin in fashion fer years. Leading trendsetters by all accounts, the ragged-ass brigade,' he laughed at the thought, and continued. 'What's call that t'other thing thee'm wearing. Looks like somebody got to it wi' a pair o' shears.'

'It's a fringed leather waistcoat, they're quite expensive,' replied Calico indignantly.

'Thee don't mean to tell I 'twas in that state when you bought it?' asked her father, feigning surprise. 'Don't tell I, 'tis the fashion.'

'Yes, and don't tell me you didn't follow the fashion in your youth,' answered Calico. 'I've heard stories about you in your motorcycle gear, riding an old Rudge, going around terrorising old ladies, making them jump back on the pavement.'

'That weren't I, that were me brother. Alus mixing us up people were. The number of times I took the blame for something 'ee did. Too smart by 'alf he was, slippery as a spring cow-pat, alus seemed to find 'n 'ole to wriggle through in the tightest of corners. I were sitting in the local pub one night, must a bin about eighteen at the time, an' in he strolls. Comes over t'me an' says, "I'll toss you for a drink our youngun, best of three. Give us a coin." As usual I lost. "Just as well you lost our youngun," he says, "'cause I 'aven't got a penny piece on I." He'd gambled wi' nothing, an' he's bin doing that ever since. Made 'imself a millionaire through taking a chance.'

Calico made herself a cup of coffee, and one for Amy, who had just come into the kitchen. 'Well I s'pose we better get on wi' milking, Mother. Thee'm a colourful pair to look at,' he said to Calico and Amy. 'Thee watch out fer plagues o' bees thinking thee'm a couple of overgrown flowers, wi' they get-ups on. When thee's finished wi' em; I'll 'ave 'em to put on me scarecrows out in longmeadow. They'll frighten off the birds for sure, spot 'em from miles away.'

'Oh, very funny,' replied Calico, 'what about your haymaking hat, now there's a sight if ever I saw one, and that navy-blue romper suit you wear in the winter.'

'Ah! but they'm functional. I'll see thee when thee gets back. Well, I'd have a hard job to miss thee in they things. Cheerio,' he said, going out of the door. 'Come on, Mother.'

'In a minute,' she turned to Calico. 'Have you enough food? I've made you a bacon sandwich for breakfast.'

'Thanks Mum. We've stacks, with all the things you've given us,' answered Calico.

'And you'll take a top-coat in case it rains. Are those back packs heavy, I can get you a lift? You will be careful,' her mother continued, fussing about her.

'Mum, stop worrying, we'll be fine.' Calico assured her. 'It's only for one night, it's not that far away and I'm taking the dogs; walking there is all part of it, like a pilgrimage.'

'Well, have a good time then dears. I'll see you tomorrow. You will be careful,' she said, repeating herself in her anxiety.

'Yes Mum, bye.'

'Bye. Take care.'

Calico and Amy sat munching the bacon sandwiches.

'It's a damn nuisance,' said Calico, frowning.

'What is?' asked Amy, looking at her.

'I've started my monthly, damn and blast; why does it always manage to pick the most unsuitable time to appear? It always seems to contrive to start when it can cause the most inconvenience. I'm not due until Monday, it's usually regular until it wants to be a nuisance. I suppose the toilet facilities will be practically non-existent. How embarrassing,' moaned Calico.

'Never mind, you'll cope,' encouraged Amy. 'We women always do; it's something we learn to live with.'

'Yes,' agreed Calico. 'We do, because we have to, we haven't been given a choice. It makes it obvious to me that God is male; if he had to suffer monthlies, he would soon have put an end to them, and found a way to populate the world without all that discomfort we women suffer. Right, we better get started.'

They put on their back packs. Calico whistled her dogs to heel, and attached their leads to their collars. She handed

Liaka over to Amy. 'Here, you can take Liaka, she's quieter than Leonie, even though she's a good deal younger. I don't expect we'll get a lift with a pair of German Shepherds at our side. But I do feel safer taking them.'

As they were going out of the farmgate into the lane, Amy referred back to their previous conversation. 'You believe in God?'

'Yes, I did fervently when I was younger. I knew he was there. For instance, one day on my way to primary school, I was wearing a mac with a detachable hood. I passed the council houses we're going by now. When I reached the village shop, I realised I had lost my hood. I thought my parents would be angry, and I started worrying. I didn't have time to go back to look for it, or I would have been late for school. Being on the horns of a dilemma, I sought help. I knelt down by the roadside, and prayed to God to find it for me. I went on to school, and didn't worry about my hood for the rest of the day, confident that I had put my problem in safe hands. God would see me through. On the way home from school, I was passing the council houses again. Two old sisters lived in the last house in the row. I used to visit them sometimes and do a bit of shopping for them. One of the sisters was calling out, and waving something in her hand at me. I went to see what she wanted, as I drew near I realised it was my hood. She said that she had seen me go past that morning. When she took the dustbin out a little later, she saw an object lying in the road. She went to investigate, found it was a hood, and thought it could be mine. She took it indoors with her in case it was. I thought it was clever of God to send her out to get my hood, after I had prayed to him. Now it seems more of a lucky coincidence. My image of God seems to be fading as I get older. I haven't got the conviction of my childhood days.'

'I know what you mean,' agreed Amy. 'We can explain things away as we get older, and gain more knowledge and insight. We don't believe so innocently any more.'

'We must start out in childhood like Adam and Eve, when they were first created by God, totally pure and innocent,' Calico suggested, thoughtfully. 'Through growing up our eyes are opened to the ways of the world, like Adam and Eve when they ate the fruit of the tree of the knowledge of good and evil.'

'Let's change the subject. It makes me shudder thinking of God, because I always associate him with death,' explained Amy. 'It's such a lovely day. I feel like a traveller of the open road, already. My whole world on my back, my faithful hound by my side; the endless sky above my head; the good earth beneath my feet; and your mother's victuals, not forgetting Mr Rolph's contributions, to look forward to at lunchtime.'

'It's an amazing sense of freedom, even if it is only for two days. Communing with nature, sleeping under the stars; surrounded by like-minded people. Soothing music floating through the air. Peace, love and harmony,' concluded Calico.

Around the halfway point of the journey, the roads became congested with vehicles and people on the move towards the festival. You could hardly see the open road any more. When Amy and Calico arrived, over a couple of hours later, at the festival site, their earlier idyllic thoughts were paling, and their spirits were flagging.

There was a surly-looking chap by the entrance gate, who approached them, and asked to see their tickets. Leonie growled a warning at him, and he backed off a step or two.

'We haven't got tickets,' replied Calico.

'Then you'll have to pay now,' he informed them. 'And make sure you got they dogs under control. I hate dogs, particularly big dogs.'

'It stated on the advert that this was a free festival,' argued Amy.

'What advert, where?' questioned the man.

'In the local paper,' answered Calico.

'You local then?' he asked.

'Yes, they both replied, wondering if that made a difference. Apparently it did.

'All right,' he said, not looking at all pleased, and standing well back out of their way. 'Go on in, but make sure those dogs don't cause any trouble.'

'What a cheek!' exclaimed Amy, when they were out of earshot. 'I wonder how much he makes out of people who don't realise it's free?'

'Leonie didn't like him. It's uncanny how dogs sense things,' commented Calico. 'People who don't like dogs; I don't mean the ones that like dogs, but don't keep one themselves, are usually not very nice characters, and are frightened of dogs because they sense this about them.'

'You better not take your dogs to the Mansion House then,' laughed Amy. 'Their throats would be sore with growling at the folk there.'

'Yes,' said Calico, smiling. 'There are some unsavoury ones, especially Mr Rolph. He makes me cringe when he's near.'

'Does the same to me,' agreed Amy. 'Whatever you do, keep out of his way. He thinks we should be grateful he gave us a job, and we ought to show our gratitude, like Sophia.'

'Like Sophia?' repeated Calico. 'This looks a good spot to pitch our tent. The water carrier and the toilet are not too far away. There's a good view over the site from here, and we'll be sheltered a bit by those trees.'

'All right, you've convinced me. We'll camp here. Don't you know about Sophia and Mr Rolph?' queried Amy.

Calico shook her head and looked blank.

'They're having an affair, to put it nicely.'

Calico looked astonished. 'How do they manage that, with so many people around?' she asked.

'When we have a banquet, Rolphie stays over, and sleeps in the spare bedroom on our floor. Then he creeps into Soppy's room when he thinks we're all asleep,' explained Amy. 'The old lecher. If you have the misfortune to be left alone with him, which I was once, but have managed to avoid since, he tells you about his Navy days and how they paid young foreign boys to "gobble them off", when they were on board ship and there were no women about.'

'What do you mean' said Calico innocently, 'gobble them off?'

Amy lowered her voice, 'He used to get young lads to suck on his willie until he came.'

This was all new to Calico. She did not like to question Amy further, even though she could not fully understand what Amy was telling her. She did not want to appear totally clueless about sex, in Amy's eyes.

'I expect that's what Sophia does to him,' continued Amy, 'To remind him of his younger days.'

Calico said nothing. She could not contribute to this conversation, so she stayed dumb. Smiling to herself as she remembered a quotation she once read, 'Stay silent and let people think you're a fool; why speak out and leave no one in any doubt?'

Amy thought she was smiling at what she had just told her, so she continued with her gossiping. 'He tries it on with all the waitresses.'

'I noticed that,' said Calico, thankful that the conversation had moved on. 'At the banquet last night, they played up to him.'

'That's because he looks after them so well. Supplies them with a meal and drinks when they're on duty; gives them food (not always left-over) and bottles of wine to take home; pays their taxi fares out of petty cash and enters it as household expenses. It's no wonder the other staff resent them, except Sophia and Maria; they get more than their fair share of perks between them anyway. Hey!' exclaimed Amy, interrupting herself, nudging Calico with her elbow, and nodding towards a group of lads. 'He's a good-looker, the one in the middle with the long black hair. I hope they camp near us.'

'Looks as though your wish is their command,' observed Calico. 'They've put their stuff down on the ground.'

'I don't think much of the choice you're left with,' laughed Amy.

'No. People are awful though aren't they? If someone isn't appealing to the eye, then we disregard them. Never finding out whether they have an appealing personality or not. In chance meetings like this, it's first impressions that count, and that means what's on show: the packaging; the face and physique. Helen of Troy might have been a right harridan inside, but there was a war waged over her outward appearance,' replied Calico sadly. She was thinking of the chauffeur as she said this, knowing that she was guilty of the human trait she had described.

'With less than two days here, there isn't time for in-depth probing into personalities,' retorted Amy. 'I'll make do with pleasing eye contact, and the rest can follow on after.'

Calico chuckled, 'You flash that cleavage about much more and you'll have eye contact all right, probably poke someone's out.'

'If you've got it don't hide it,' laughed Amy, standing up straight, hands on hips, and her chest pushed out to its fullest extent.

'That's good. Stay like that, the dogs are in the shade now,' remarked Calico.

'Cheeky cow,' returned Amy. 'Still, at least that chap's noticed me.'

'I'm not surprised. He probably thought the sky had clouded over as well.'

Amy beamed falsely, and said through clenched teeth, 'He's coming across.'

Calico watched the tall slim dark-haired youth. He did not stride manfully out as he walked, but came towards them with short awkward steps.

'Hi,' he greeted them. 'That's two fine-looking dogs you have there. Black and grey is quite an unusual colour for a dog.'

'Bitch,' corrected Calico.

'Pardon,' he looked at her quickly, and then he smiled. 'Oh! Can I stroke them, or do they get nasty with strangers?'

'Only on command,' Calico replied.

'I'd love a German Shepherd this colour,' he said, making a fuss of Liaka. 'It's a shame she's long-coated and you can't show her. She's a lovely girl.'

'You could be in luck. She was mated a few weeks ago, it's too early to tell yet, but hopefully she's taken,' Calico informed him.

'Will they be pedigree?' he asked.

'Yes,' replied Calico. 'The stud dog has quite an impressive pedigree; several British champions, a couple of international champions and a Crufts supreme champion, in his background. He belongs to a friend, that's the only reason I could afford to use him. Liaka has a few champions in her background, but most of them are trained working dogs for the police and the Services. She was bred by a vet, who was trying to breed dogs with good hips and get rid of hip dysplasia. She has a lovely temperament as well. So between them they should throw a few good short-coats.'

'Okay, you've sold one to me. I want a dog for showing. I've just had the one I was bringing on put to sleep. He had cancer and I couldn't let him go on suffering. He was only eighteen months old, and already had two challenge certificates and three reserve ones,' he said sadly.

'Didn't you know he had cancer?' questioned Calico. 'Couldn't you tell it was thinner or something?'

'No. He looked fine until about a month before his death,' he answered her. 'When he was a puppy I felt a lump on his side, at the bottom of one of his ribs. I asked the vet about it, when I took him in for his inoculations at about ten weeks old. He assured me it was nothing to worry about, it was the way the bone was growing. The lump stayed about the same size for over a year. Then I noticed it was getting bigger. I went to another vet, and he thought it could be a tumour. He kept the dog in overnight to X-ray, and then operate to remove it. When I returned the next morning to fetch the dog, the vet told me the lump was cancerous, there was nothing he could do, it had been left too long. He advised me to put him to sleep.'

'How awful,' commiserated Calico. 'You can look the litter over, to see if there's one puppy good enough for showing.'

He unzipped a black leather purse that was swinging from his belt, and took out a business card. 'Here,' he said, handing the card to Calico. 'Give me a ring when she's whelped, and we'll arrange a meet to see the litter.'

'Yes, I'll do that,' Calico assured him.

'Okay, thanks. Have a good time here, I'll probably see you around some time later. By the way you know my name, what's yours?'

'I'm Calico and this is Amy.'

'Right, bye for now then. I'll be seeing you.' He walked back to join his friends.

'You were quiet,' Calico chided Amy. 'I thought you fancied him. At least you know his name and telephone number now, and that he's a nice person.'

'That's no good to me,' retorted Amy, sullenly. Calico regarded her; she thought she would have been pleased with this information.

'It's no good to me. He's not interested in me,' persisted Amy.

'How do you know that?' demanded Calico.

'Because he's not into women,' said Amy, simply.

'Not into women,' Calico repeated stupidly.

'He's of the other persuasion, you know.'

A look of enlightenment came over Calico's face. 'What a damn shame. He's so handsome, and seems gentle and caring. There's a case in point about what we were saying just now. Deceptive outward appearances.'

'Just my luck,' said Amy bitterly. 'The dogs have had the most attention so far. Hand me the bag of food and the bottles of wine. I'm going to indulge. Come Bacchus fill my mournful soul to overflow, and drown my sorrows in your sweet-tasting breath.'

'Oh, don't be so melancholic,' reproved Calico. 'What's one amongst so many. If you drink too much of that wine you'll never find another chap, because you'll only be seeing them in pairs. Why not wait and drink it this evening?' 'It's my theatrical up-bringing that makes me melodramatic,' laughed Amy. 'You're right. I'll leave the wine till later. I'd like to have seen Rolphie's puzzled face, if he did count the wine bottles he was pinching. What wine have we here, I grabbed a red one and a white one. This one's got a nice label, Rieussec 1949; I remember that from last night. Bit old though, still that's supposed to be a good thing for wine. I don't remember this one, 1959 Haut-

Brion. The old sod must have bought it in specially for him, and his hangers-on.'

'Shall we go nearer the stage when we've eaten, and watch the groups?' suggested Calico. 'We can hear them from here; but I wouldn't mind seeing them in person,' Amy agreed.

Calico surveyed the scene while she ate. Several more people had arrived and set up camp since they had been there. *All these different types of people gathered together*, she thought. Hippies with flowered colourful clothes, lots of hair, and bare feet, all smiling as they wandered past. Students, in T-shirts advertising their varsity on the front, Levis and baseball boots, talking intensely together. To the left of them was an expensive-looking tent, belonging to a group dressed in suede and leather trousers, with silk shirts. They were emptying the contents of an enormous hamper, and quaffing champagne. To the right was a group of hell's angels, wearing jeans that looked as though they could stand up in their own right, and sleeveless jean jackets in much the same condition. They had unwashed, unkempt hair and beards, wore dark glasses and sinister expressions. These four groups were the most prominent ones; everyone else seemed to fit in somewhere in between. It was amazing that people who would not want to be associated with each other, in normal circumstances, came together as one under the influence of this festival.

Calico could make out the stage from her vantage point. Chiefly because it was surrounded by a technicolour sea; a myriad of bright colours bobbing and swaying about with the flow of the music. She looked beyond the festival fields into the distance. Her eyes rested on St Michael's Mount at the end of the valley. Standing serene, peaceful and immutable through the centuries. The holy landmark that must have watched over the coming and going of thousands: Britons, Romans, Saxons, Normans, Celts, Druids; steeped in history. Calico regarding it felt a sense of awe, and shuddered, as she realised how transitory the individual time of a human life is compared to its surroundings. Calico tried to snap herself out of such thoughts. It wasn't wise to think too deeply about these things; to dwell on them could make you depressed. You are given your allotted span, you cannot change it, so you have to make the best of it: it is the same for everybody.

Her gran told her, 'You don't have to be happy in this life, you just have to get through it to reach heaven.'

'But what about hell?' Calico asked her.

'There is no hell. We're living it. Do you imagine there could be a worse life than this for some people?' she answered.

'Calico,' Amy said, and repeated it louder. 'Calico, you're off thinking again aren't you? Your brain must be crowded out by now, let's go and look around the trading stalls; we might find you a new one, they sell all sorts.'

'That's a good idea,' retorted Calico. 'I could do with a spare. What do you think its shelf life would be, or would it be better to store it in the freezer?'

'No, because then your mother would make it into brawn along with the pigs' brains, don't suppose they differ that much,' giggled Amy, and then laughed out loud at the absurdity of it. Calico joined in. The dogs looked uneasy, it was one of the things they could not do, so they did not take kindly to the noise. The laughter was good for Calico, it sent her earlier morbid thoughts winging out of her head, towards St Michael's Mount from where they had originated.

They left their tent pitched, but packed up everything else and took it with them. They made their way to the field that contained all the stalls, weaving their way between the crowds, getting stopped several times by people requesting if they had any spare drugs, or if they wanted to purchase any. Their answer being negative in both cases.

'It's a mug's game,' stated Amy, 'taking drugs. I've seen what they can do, a lot of people in my mother's circle, you know, creative sorts, take them. Ages them terribly.'

'My mother told me drugs are for people who don't want to face up to the reality of life, who need a prop to get them through it,' said Calico. '"Like the washing, that's propped up to dry," I told her trying to be obtuse. She replied by agreeing and using it as an example. "In a way. When you prop up the washing line, the washing is lifted up high, it dances about in the wind, as if it didn't have a care in the world. When you take the prop away and bring it down to earth, it hangs there still and lifeless, then it's put away in dark closets. You use your common sense, and stay away from drugs. You don't need them, it's a coward's way out. Nothing is so bad on this earth that it can't be faced." That's the advice she gave me.'

'Yes,' said Amy thoughtfully, continuing the theme. 'The more often the washing needs to be propped up, the more frayed and worn it becomes. Until finally it's so threadbare, the pegs are unable to hold on to it when an extra fierce gust of wind comes along and snatches it up skyward; it never comes down again, never gets returned to the dark closet.'

They finally got as near as they could to the main stage. Hawkwind were playing, the group was one of Calico's favourites. They sat down on the ground to watch and listen. Marc Bolan appeared next; there was a rumour travelling around that Jimi Hendrix was booked to appear, but nobody could seem to verify it, or say what time he would be on stage. Amy suggested after they had watched several more bands perform, that they went back to their tent: because she didn't think she would be able to find it later when it got dark.

On returning to their tent, they found many more people had managed to squeeze tents in between the ones that were there in the morning. Calico thought to anyone gazing down upon the scene, it must look like a kaleidoscope of canvas molehills erupting from the ground.

'I don't like this,' whispered Calico perturbed. 'It's too crowded now. Can't we camp somewhere else?'

'What do you suggest? All the fields will be the same,' replied Amy.

'I know the farmer, Mr Brown, who owns the adjoining fields,' proffered Calico. 'He buys Dad's beefers from him. He offered to let me camp on his land, when he knew I was coming here; but I declined. I wanted to be on the site and soak in the atmosphere. Now all these people frighten me, it's so overpowering. I'm not used to being so closely surrounded.'

'All right,' said Amy, beginning to dismantle the tent. 'I feel a bit uneasy myself and I'm used to crowds.'

They packed up the tent and walked into the next field, which was just as jam-packed with people as the one they had left. 'We'll have to go back on to the road, and enter the next field by the roadside gate. That must be Mr Brown's land because there is no gate leading to it from this field. Which means it doesn't belong to the chap who is holding the festival,' reasoned Calico.

When they entered the field they discovered a few more people were on the same wavelength, and had already pitched their tents. 'Oh good!' exclaimed Amy. 'We're not completely isolated, we still have some company. That's better isn't it?'

There was a stream running through the top of this field. Calico caught sight of several nude bodies cavorting about in the water, and sitting on the little wooden bridge that crossed over the stream. Pale figures among natures rich greens and browns. Calico could equate herself with them. She had often gone skinny-dipping in the river near her home, when she was a little girl, before shyness and embarrassment took over. She did not realise that this was a new experience for these city-dwellers, that country-folk took for granted; the feel of nature all around them, shades of colour and clean air, instead of sludge-grey and exhaust fumes.

As Calico and Amy put up their tent, the music wafted up to them. They were about halfway up the side of the valley, and could still see the stage; at this angle St Michael's Mount no longer hovered over it, but stood proudly to the left. They sat down and dug into their backpacks, to see what food was left. Calico spread it out, while Amy opened the bottles of wine. Calico's mother had given her a large game pie, which Calico gave to the dogs. She couldn't eat anything she might have seen running free on the farm. The dogs had no such qualms and made short work of it, then sat waiting for the next delicacy that might befall them.

There was the food Amy had salvaged the previous night: a plastic tub of cold chicken curry with apricots and cashew nuts, which was a favourite of Calico's. Homemade crusty bread and farmhouse butter. Thick slices of home-cooked ham, to make into sandwiches. Slices of cake, date and walnut, cherry and almond, carrot and brazil nut; all made by her mother's own (from years of toil on the farm, it would be an untruth to describe them as fair) hands. Wedges of cheese and some fruit.

They ate, drank, and talked; felt peaceful, warm and relaxed, as though their bones had all melted together. Calico wanted to share this moment with Charles. He stayed stubbornly shading her thoughts, she could not dismiss him from her mind.

One of the surrounding groups had lit a campfire, and invited the select company present to join them around it.

Calico saved the fruit and cheese for breakfast, and put it in the tent. Then she and Amy shared their repast with the others. There was plenty of enthusing from them, when they sampled the homemade fare. The dogs did well out of the prepared food the others had brought with them, which they threw away when they tasted Calico's.

Today was June 21st, the summer solstice. The people gathered around the flickering flames, observing the fire's colours mirrored in the fingers of red-gold sun, disappearing behind St Michael's Mount, as many wanderers before them, through the centuries, must have similarly on this day. They watched the sky through all its hues, talking quietly together feeling reverence to nature in her evening shroud, until it became quite dark, and the first star of the night had been joined by its fellows. They heaped more wood upon the fire, as the night grew chill, nature's primary heater had gone down, so a secondary one had to be stoked up to compensate. The dark night crept further down around them. The stars shining overhead reflected the glow of the faces in the firelight.

The music had finished. There were sounds of shrieking and screaming, as people tried to find the way back to their tents, by the weak light of the moon, falling over bodies and tent ropes, leaving chaos in their wake.

One of the people around the campfire began strumming a guitar. A couple of the others sang along with him, it was rather a doleful tune. Some more people joined the group, and handed round drugs, so Amy and Calico thought this an opportune moment to creep away. They could still hear the singing from their tent, but they were tired and relaxed and soon fell asleep.

The dogs spent an uneasy night. There was too much disturbance around for them to relax for long. Likewise, the wildlife of the area: the badgers, foxes, hares, rabbits, owls, bats, mice, and deer among them. No one saw hide nor hair of them over the long weekend; not even on the mystical night of the summer solstice. As if forewarned, they had vacated the area, and left it to human activity.

But they were there, watching, unseen from afar, until they could reclaim their territory.

The sun ascended, sending golden streaks along the skyline, to intermingle with the silvery threads of cloud which a slight wind was chasing across the blue background, as if to hurry them on their way.

Calico and Amy had gone to sleep easily, but when they awoke from their deep sleep, they became aware of the hardness of the ground beneath them. They could not nestle into it, it fought against the contours of their bodies, unyielding, uncompromising. At the first speck of light, insects were on the move; ignoring the fact that there were obstructions in their pathway. Calico, lying there, found she was in the middle of the insect equivalent of a motorway, and got up. She let the dogs out of the tent. They bounded up to the stream with Calico and Amy following.

When they arrived at the wooden bridge, they discovered the water was not fit for them to wash in, nor for the dogs to drink. Several people had been using it as a toilet. So they walked further to find the animals a drink. About three fields later, they found a spring bubbling up through the ground. Pure unadulterated water, crystal clear and God-given, exactly the variety the dogs preferred.

They had a good view over the festival site from this field. People were beginning to surface from their tents, like rabbits emerging from their burrows, to greet another day. In a matter of minutes the scene before them was transformed from a dormant peaceful setting to an ant-hill of activity. People were scurrying off in all directions to find wood for their fires, water for their morning drink, and a place to relieve themselves after finding the toilets overcrowded.

Retracing their steps, Calico and Amy arrived back at their tent in time to share a hot drink with the people they had met the previous night. Whoever had brewed-up over the fire had rekindled it from yesterday's ashes. 'St Michael's Mount stands out clear this morning,' remarked one lad, whose name was William. Calico had noticed him the previous night, and thought how pleasant he seemed. He had dark blonde hair, brown eyes, and a sense of humour that matched her own. Then he told her he was a farmer's son, which put a black mark against him from Calico's viewpoint.

'Yes,' answered Calico in agreement. 'And the noises from the festival site are plainly heard. Another bad sign.'

'What do you mean, a bad sign?' Amy wanted to know.

'A bad sign for what?' joined in a man called John, who had his arm loosely about Amy's shoulders. He had tried to get Amy interested in him all evening, and this morning it looked as though he had succeeded in his quest.

'It's weather lore,' explained Calico. 'My gran told me, when distant objects stand out clear and plain, sometimes with a sort of glow about them, and distant noises are heard more distinctly, it means that rain is coming. It's because the excessive moisture in the air makes it unusually clear. Also the sky is covered with "mares' tails", that's those thread-like clouds.' She pointed skywards. They all looked up, and then across to St Michael's Mount to verify her statement.

'But it might not come to much, because the sun went down with such a fiery hue,' consoled William. 'It shouldn't spoil the day. Are you staying another night?' He directed this question at Calico.

'No, we're leaving later this afternoon,' replied Calico. 'Amy has to get back to Brydle by this evening.'

'So am I. I can give you a lift,' offered William.

'Where do you live?' inquired Calico.

'Castle Moreton,' he answered.

'But it's out of your way to—'

'I can give you a lift,' interrupted John, 'I go your way.' His ears had pricked up when Calico had mentioned Amy. He listened in on their conversation, to see if he might hear something he could turn to his advantage, and this was it.

'Oh!' exclaimed Calico, surprised at his intervention. She looked at Amy for her voice on the matter. Amy looked at John.

'I live in the Hampton district of Brydle, so I could take you back,' ventured John.

'We can drop Calico off on the way.'

'But you haven't got a—' one of John's mates started to say.

John silenced him with a look and cut in quickly, 'I can borrow your van, Muscles, can't I.' It was more of a statement than a question.

'Yeah, I s'pose,' he growled in reply. 'Shan't need it today.'

'Well, that's settled,' said John cheerfully.

John and his mates had arrived late yesterday afternoon. They started drinking straight away, and then gone into the festival fields. John came back and sat by the campfire talking to Amy. His mates returned when the music finished – they were the ones who had handed around the drugs. Calico had to admit that they frightened her. They were so loud and aggressive that she did not know how to handle them or what to say to them. She was relieved when she realised only John was going with them. Muscles handed over the van keys, then he and the rest of his group headed towards the hole they had made in the hedge adjoining the festival site. They had ripped out and uprooted young trees, bushes and brambles, carelessly for their own convenience, never thinking that it was the habitat of wildlife, that the young trees would grow into tall dignified specimens, and that someone would have to repair the hedge they had destroyed, before cattle were put in the field.

There was an open-air service outside the church tent. Calico and Amy decided to attend. 'Being so close to nature, watching it at first hand, makes me believe there could be a God,' admitted Amy. 'And it frightens me even more to think what sort of being He must be, to have master-minded the Cosmos.' Then Amy did her usual quick change of subject, whenever she started thinking about God too deeply, by finishing with, 'What do you think of John?'

'He seems better than his mates,' answered Calico evasively.

'He's good-looking, don't you think?' persisted Amy. 'Sort of Italianish, dark and sensual.'

'And short,' concluded Calico.

A light drizzle of rain fell at first, the kind that settles on to clothing, quietly creeping inwards to the skin. By the end of the service it was raining harder and their clothes were quite damp. It did not help, that at frequent intervals, the dogs shook away the droplets of moisture clinging to their shaggy coats.

Walking back to their tent, they passed near the main stage. People were dancing around in the mud. They had scant clothes on, and you could hardly tell black from white as they slipped and slithered about in the oozy brownness. Calico had never seen so many coloured folk in one place. There was only one in her village, the result of a liaison between a young village girl and a coloured American airman.

The sun broke through as they were departing. Calico looked back on the scene from the van window: St Michael's Mount rose majestic above the surrounding countryside, a rainbow arched out on either side of it, framing the festival site, the colours co-ordinating with the many displayed below against a background of greens and browns; a mystical aura encircling all. It was a spiritual experience, a social leveller, participated in and enjoyed by rich and poor alike, equal while within.

Chapter Five

Sadistic Tendencies

He jests at scars that never felt a wound.

Shakespeare

The morning after the festival, Calico and Amy were in the Mansion House setting the breakfast table. Sophia was downstairs in the kitchen, pretending to be busy as usual. Amy told Calico that John had asked for a date, when he dropped her off at the Mansion House, and she was seeing him on her day off, which hardly came as any surprise to Calico. What did come as a surprise to her was that there had been no mention of the Lord Mayor's starched underwear. On confiding this fact to Amy, the latter replied, 'I thought it would be hushed-up, seeing as it was darling Sophia the accusing finger would be pointed towards. After all, it couldn't possibly be us. Mr Rolph knew that the door to the downstairs was locked Friday evening; even though he daren't admit it. We left then, I returned last night and you early this morning. So though he may suspect us, there's damn all he can do about it. But watch your back from now on, he'll be trying to get even. Especially since a woman is being employed part-time, to see to the Mayor's personal laundry.'

'That was quick, how do you know that?'

'The gardener asked me, if it was right what Charles had told him about the Mayor wanting someone to do her laundry; because his wife was interested,' replied Amy.

'My gosh!' exclaimed Calico. 'What a grapevine creeps around here.'

'I bet Soppy is upset. Old Rolphie couldn't swing it for her this time,' said Amy gleefully. 'I wonder if she'll withdraw his visiting rights over this, no suckie, no – Sophia!'

'Why no finish, molto troppo yak yak yak, not work yak yak yak.' said Sophia nastily, and then flounced out muttering to herself.

'Off to report to Rolphie no doubt,' said Amy, making a face in the direction Sophia had gone. 'She's only a parlourmaid, the same as us. Just because she's been here for years, it doesn't mean she has seniority over us. She thinks she has though.'

'Well let her think on,' snapped Calico. 'The mockers have been put on any chance of advancement she had.'

The rest of the morning passed uneventfully. It was Amy's half-day, so she went off duty at eleven. Calico was working the split shift, morning from seven to one, evening from seven to ten. They agreed to meet in the city centre to go shopping, that afternoon. Amy bought a mock snakeskin mini-skirt and waistcoat, to wear for her date with John the next day. Calico could only afford a pair of black seamed tights.

That evening the chauffeur returned after taking the Mayor to the Council House, to see Calico. He had been trying to see her alone ever since the evening he had kissed her. She had objected slightly at first, and then seemed to give herself up to him. He wanted a repeat performance.

He entered the kitchen. Calico was concentrating on getting the seams of her tights straight. She did not notice him until he was standing in front of her.

'I'll help you with that,' he said, meaningfully, his eyes holding hers, his lips slightly parted, his hands on their way down to offer assistance. Calico felt his nearness affect her body. 'No thank you,' she said curtly, her cheeks tinged with red.

Then an Italian contraceptive (if there is such a thing) appeared in the shape of Sophia, who took up residence in the window seat behind the kitchen table and settled herself like a bird on its eggs, prepared for a long stay. Calico and Charles knew Sophia was intending to remain there to make sure there was no chance of them being alone.

'I must see you,' Charles implored her, quietly.

'No,' hissed Calico. 'It's not right.'

'Please, just once,' Charles begged, whispering.

This is no good, he thought. He could not plead his case under these circumstances. 'I won't give up. I want you too much,' and with this line he departed.

Sophia got up from her seat and walked across the kitchen with a smirk on her face. She returned to the staff sitting room, mission accomplished, Charles had gone. With a took of triumph on her face, Sophia stretched out comfortably on the chaise longue, and continued to gorge herself on the chocolates Mr Rolph had procured for her. Watching the colour television, (colour being a new innovation), Mr Rolph had bought for her as a peace-offering after the events of the weekend, with childish delight.

Calico was relieved Sophia had intervened, she did not know what to do about Charles. She knew it would be wrong to go out with a married man, but she liked the feelings that coursed through her body at the sight of him. She wanted to follow her heart, and experience what it was like to be with a man, who brought out the physical side of you. If he managed to see her alone, she was powerless to refuse him. If he turned to her with that longing, almost desperate look in his eyes, she would be malleable in his hands.

Calico did not realise, being a newcomer to the manipulation game played by the sexes, that Charles always used this tactic as openers in his affairs. The seemingly single-minded 'I want you; I've never wanted anyone as much as I want you; let me see you just once; I need to see you; I have to see you'; (notice the word love never creeps in); eventually wears the victim down. It makes them feel guilty, that they should be the cause of such suffering and anguish to this man; and thus the central focus of all his desires gives in. After the first date and more emotional spillage falling from his lips, they are captivated.

Calico's feelings towards Charles had not been confided to Amy. Being on her own so often throughout her childhood, she was used to thinking for herself, without discussing matters with other people. The next day, her habit of putting her thoughts into action without consulting anybody else, led her into a situation that created the most odd-shaped, odd-coloured piece that she could not fit into her patchwork at all.

Calico decided to get her father a pair of binoculars, similar to the consort's, for his birthday. She thought that on her afternoon shift she would slip upstairs to the consort's room, to find out the make and number of his binoculars which he kept on his dressing-chest. The Mayor and the consort had functions to attend all day; Mr Rolph had informed her that they would not return until late so she did not have to make them afternoon tea, she was to clean and sort out the pantry to keep herself occupied.

Calico knew that the Lord Mayor's quarters were out of bounds to the staff, when they were unoccupied in the afternoon. She did not think it would matter, just this once. No one would know, and she was not going to damage anything. She needed the make of the binoculars to find out how much she had to save up to buy them. They would be useful to her father. He could stand at the back door, and check the number of heifers and steers in the bottom field without having to make the daily trek across two fields to make sure they were all still present and correct.

With her mind on other things, Calico opened the door to the consort's room. She stood as if turned to stone, not knowing what to do and totally unprepared for the scene in front of her. There sat on the bed smoking, wearing skin tight leather pants covered in studs and nothing else, was Tryphena. She thought at first the housekeeper was sat on the bed; then she realised she was sat on somebody, who looked remarkably like the consort.

'Hi Cal,' said Tryphena, not in the least perturbed. 'What are you doing here?'

Calico wanted to ask her what she was doing here, but as she could see what she was doing, it seemed a daft question. Calico did wonder why the consort was tied to the bed, after all he was hardly likely to get away with Tryphena sat on him. The scene was beyond Calico's understanding, but she could not ignore it, could not will her eyes away. 'I came to find the make of the consort's binoculars,' she managed finally to say. 'I was going to buy my father a pair like them for his next birthday so that he can count his young stock from the back door, without having to walk down to check on them.' Calico knew she was gabbling on, she could not help it. If she stopped talking she would have to face the sight before her eyes. Why was the consort gagged? It was like a painting in front of her: the more she looked, the more detail she noticed: like the colour of the consort's face.

'Should he be that colour?' she ventured.

'Don't worry about him,' answered Tryphena carelessly. 'He enjoys it. This is how he gets his pleasure. He's a masochist you see.' Calico did not see, she had never encountered that word before, but she would not admit it. Tryphena continued talking, 'Sometimes I tread on him and bounce up and down on his bottom now and then, he likes that: it's quite painful when his penis is hard. That's why I have to gag him, so whoever's on duty can't hear him moaning and groaning.'

'What are those red marks?' inquired Calico, who still could not quite believe what she was seeing and hearing.

'That's from the whipping,' explained Tryphena. 'It takes a bit of effort on my part, I rest halfway through and sit on him. That's what the studs are for on my pants so they dig into him. He has to be in constant pain for the hour, or he says he hasn't got his money's worth. I have a ciggie and stub it out on his ass; it gives me a chuckle when I see him wince as he sits down at an official dinner. I have to finish off his whipping, you can watch if you like; though I won't be able to talk to you, I have to scold him, and whisper obscenities to him while I'm doing it. He did want me to wear coarse net crutchless pants, and sit on his face to half suffocate him while I whipped him; but I draw the line at that. It's far too dangerous. I know how much my customers can take, I push them to the limit, but never over it.'

'Your customers?' queried Calico faintly.

'Yes. He isn't the only one. Good grief you don't actually think I am a housekeeper? You do, I can tell by your face. What a sheltered life you've led. How awful, it must be quite incomprehensible to you what I'm doing. I've been rabbitting on thinking you knew what I was on about. Well, you've certainly had an eye-opener this afternoon. All you wanted to find out was the make of a pair of binoculars,' laughed Tryphena.

The situation was highly amusing to her. Her employment as a housekeeper at the Lord Mayor's was only a respectable cover, she was actually employed to satisfy the sexual desires of the local dignitaries, businessmen, and visiting guests of the city council. She had a reliable group of people whose services could be called upon, who specialised in different sexual areas. She could be loosely described as a 'madam'.

Tryphena had been brought up as a spoilt child of a seemingly wealthy family, with good social connections. At twenty her world collapsed around her when her father died. Unbeknown to his family, he was in debt, and everything had to be sold off. No longer cushioned, Tryphena had to earn her living. But what could she do? Only skilled in social niceties, she lived off her family's good connections for a while, and travelled around. She stayed with a great-uncle in India, a cousin in Africa; an Honourable in Rome; a count in Florence; a marquis in Venice; a shipping magnate in Greece; a chain-store owner in the Loire Valley; her mother's hairdresser in Spain, and so on, until she had worn out all her welcomes, and exhausted all her supply of contacts. She then returned to London. Here she found the saying 'every woman is sitting on a fortune' to be absolutely true. But there was too much competition in London, she was a small fish in a big pool, and there were sharks to contend with.

When Tryphena heard a rumour through the 'good connections' that she still fostered, about the good time one of them had when visiting Brydle on business; she made discreet inquiries. She found that it was taking too much of the council secretary's time to find hostesses to keep the people they did business with sweet. She offered her services, and was accepted. There had not been a housekeeper at the Lord Mayor's for several years: when the last one had left, her duties were divided between the head butler, parlourmaids and cleaners. With his inspired deviousness, which had kept him his position for so long, the council secretary installed Tryphena as the housekeeper at the Mansion House, on a fixed salary (with annual increments), and the rest of the money as cash in hand. The associates Tryphena called upon for their services were given the job descriptions of waitresses, wine waiters, temporary cleaners, catering assistants, and they were billed to the council under fictitious agency names. Tryphena naturally assumed that the legitimate staff suspected the set-up but as nothing could be proved, and they wanted to keep their jobs, they kept quiet about it.

Calico was still rooted to the spot staring stupefied.

'Well carry on then,' urged Tryphena.

'Carry on?' repeated Calico feebly.

'Find out the make of the binoculars. That's what you came here to do. Only look sharp there's a love, I've got work to do. He's probably gone soft by now, I'll have to put in some extra work to get him hard again. I haven't got an awful lot of time left before the Lord Mayor returns, so I'll have to work fast. Whew! I'm going to be pooped, and I've got two more to do tonight,' finished Tryphena matter-of-factly.

Calico crossed over to the dressing-chest and wrote down the information she needed. She could not take all this in. 'Two more,' she heard herself saying. 'Two more who like that, two more like him.'

'It's to do with their upbringing you know: nanny, then public school, university, the services. Need to be disciplined and dominated to get their excitement, sexual stimuli,' replied Tryphena flippantly. 'One of them likes to be tied in an upright position and whipped all round. The other likes to be gagged and bound very tightly and left. So I can deal with them both in adjoining rooms, makes my job easier.'

Calico wished she had not asked. The more she heard the odder it seemed.

'Do you enjoy doing that?' Calico inquired, knowing she would not be able to bring herself to do it, even with the person's consent, and however much they begged her.

'It doesn't worry me,' admitted Tryphena. 'It makes me a lot of money quickly so I can afford to travel the world, wear designer clothes, eat in expensive restaurants, drive fast cars, and live in the style to which I used to be accustomed until I can find a wealthy titled husband to look after me.'

Calico departed, and thought about what she had just witnessed. Believing in God, she could not work out how it figured in the scheme of things. She did not condemn the consort or Tryphena. It was not up to her to judge. If no one came to any harm, and they were both consenting adults, then it was really no one else's business, Calico decided. But she could not vanquish it from her mind and for the rest of the shift she wondered about it. According to Tryphena it was the well-educated ones from wealthy families who craved that sort of treatment to get their kicks and satisfy themselves. More to be pitied than repulsed by. Something instilled in them from the cradle, and clung on to all their life, a dependency. As some people were hooked on drugs, alcohol, or cigarettes, they were hooked on this.

It was difficult for Calico to understand. Strong sexual feelings had not been aroused in her yet. All she knew was the physical reaction she felt whenever she saw Charles. She had no parallel on which to base an analysis. Her mother had never ventured far on the subject of sex. Her gran explained a little further, when Calico, playing by the cowstall, watched fascinated as a man put on a long rubber glove, unrolled it past his elbow, and pushed his arm up a cow's back-end. Her father appeared at that moment and sent her inside. She questioned her gran, who proceeded to explain to her about artificial insemination; coldly and clinically; never touching upon the subjects of passion and romance as a part of the reproduction process.

Tryphena, on the other hand, knew about sex and men's needs. Her parents for all their outward show, were not in love with each other. Tryphena's mother would dole out her sexual favours only when she wanted something: a fur coat, jewellery, a trip to Europe, and so on. Her husband, finally tired of this behaviour, satisfied himself elsewhere. Tryphena as a child, did not understand why Mummy was often alone in the double bed, when she visited her in the early hours of the morning. Yet her father was always present at the breakfast table. She accepted this when young, in later years it upset her. She thought of her father as two people; the day-time daddy who indulged her and whom she loved dearly; and the night-time daddy who cultivated his baser instincts and she despised, never thinking that her mother was partly to blame for using sex as a bargaining power. She sold her services to her husband for jewels, clothes and cars, just as Tryphena was selling hers to men for cash to purchase the same.

To Tryphena her mother was the injured party, who bravely bore the wrong done to her with a martyred air. She set her up on a pedestal, and put her alongside all the tragic heroines she read about. It was only when her father died and her mother went to live with a friend of the family, known as 'Uncle' Jake, that Tryphena realised that the shopping trips Mummy went on with Aunt Emilina, were really passion trips with 'Uncle' Jake. When you find out both your parents have been living a lie, supposedly for your sake, it's hard to trust anyone again. Sex seemed to be at the root of the problem between her parents so now it could help her get what she wanted out of life, it could be turned to her advantage. Sex to Tryphena was manipulation, pain, hurt and suffering. She had not come across the loving, giving, pleasureable kind yet.

Calico had always been a little in awe of Tryphena. She seemed so sophisticated and worldly-wise. Now Calico felt equal to her. When we find a skeleton in someone's cupboard it does not change them in any way, but it does change our attitude towards them. Calico had gained confidence from what she had seen, and felt able to approach Tryphena, a thing she would never have dared to do before in case of a rebuff. She wanted to know about the places Tryphena had been, the things she had seen, the people she had met.

Calico had read about these places, but had never known anyone who had first-hand knowledge of them, until now. She had seen pictures of their architecture, their paintings, their sculptures, their frescoes, and read about their history in books her father bought as job lots, at the farm sales he attended. He did not actually bid specifically for the books: it was usually an old clock or a piece of china his wife wanted, that had been put in the same lot as the books. Without even realising it, he had built up a considerable collection of fine classical books.

There was so much Tryphena seemed to know about art and literature, and the things Calico wanted to learn more about. Her entry into the Mansion House, with its paintings and antiques, had awakened an awareness in Calico towards the beauty of man-made objects. Before, the natural beauty God had created had satisfied her, as she walked through it in the countryside, and saw, smelt, and heard it all around her. Now she realised that man had worked upon this natural beauty, had extended it and had enhanced it in a different way, using the skill God had given him.

Thinking about these things had removed her thoughts from the scene she had previously witnessed, but not blotted it out completely. Calico was glad she was going home for a couple of weeks. She needed the familiarity of home life to surround her. She needed time to put the last few months in perspective. So many things she had heard, seen, and felt, that had opened her eyes to the adult world, and she was afraid of entering into it.

Chapter Six

Home and Hay-Making

Calico had taken up her position at the Mansion House on the understanding that she could have two weeks off in July to return home to help with the hay-making. Wherever she was, whatever she was doing, she was expected to help with the hay-making on the farm. Many an expectant, starry-eyed romance became a non-starter when her beau realised he was expected to labour for love, during hay-making time.

To her friends summer holidays were long relaxing days soaking up the sun. To her they were warm, weak orange squash and sweat. All her friends returned to school sporting suntans; they could undress in the sun and drink the sunshine into their bare skin. She had to dress up for hay-making. Unless you were driving the tractors most of the time, protective clothing was advisable: a straw hat or headscarf to keep the dust and hayseeds out of the hair; a long-sleeved shirt and jeans to protect the skin from the scratchy dry-grass stalks; baseball boots to protect the feet and ankles when walking about over the haybales; and a pair of gloves to prevent the balertwine around the hay cutting in to the hands, when you lifted the bales about.

Artists painted idyllic scenes of hay gathering on farms, making it look like an enjoyable pastime. Calico knew differently from experience, though she had to admit, from her vague remembrances of the past, it did seem easier when the hay was sent up on an elevator to make the hayrick, instead of compacted into tight carryable oblongs, spewed out by a machine.

This was the only time she felt resentment towards Nature. Having grown up surrounded by Mother Earth's marvels, she still never failed to find delight in them. A new born calf; wild flowers; the hues of sunset and sunrise; the stars twinkling overhead in a blue-black velvet cloth, accompanied by the changing faces of the moon; the landscape altered by a fall of snow; mushrooms that sprang up overnight like magic; all the varying shades of green, colouring the leaves of trees and plants and hedges; the scent of flowers; the sound of birdsong; the feel of a summer breeze gently playing with the strands of her hair and caressing her face. She loved walking barefoot through cool grass in warm weather. Lying with the soil beneath her, the long grass surrounding her, like a hare in its form: hidden from the world, gazing up at the sky. Imagining the clouds into shapes of animals, or people's faces or scenes of life. A child of nature. Enjoying simple pleasures that are free, God-given, there for everyone who has a mind to make use of them.

But Nature is a hard taskmaster, and for these two weeks Calico was a reluctant slave to the soil. The grass was ready for mowing, so cut, dried and gathered in, it had to be. Her father (with his hands as hard as iron from his life's labour for love), was more a devotee than a slave to the soil. He had the right temperament for farming: patience, tenacity and a philosophical attitude to life. These were the main ingredients needed when battling against the weather, soils, crops, breeds, and Nature at her worst. The ability to put failures behind you was essential, like a bad harvest or a dead calf. Shrugging his shoulders, Calico's father would say, 'Where there's livestock there's dead stock.' No two days were alike, the only consistency on the farm was the twice daily milking of the cows. There was hedging and ditching, ploughing, hay-making or silaging, muck-spreading, crop harvesting, repairing the machinery, gardening; always something to do, seven days a week, every week of the year. The farmer had to be a nutritionist as well, to ensure his animals gave of their best. Then he started to interfere with Mother Nature, by getting rid of the old bull, and allowing the artificial insemination chap to call. But Mother Nature got her own back when the bulls used, produced calves too big for the smaller breeds of cow. Calving created a lot of trouble for the unfortunate cow and the farmer, often resulting in a dead calf and sometimes a dead cow. Nature has things all reasoned out, and cannot be ignored, except at your own risk. She fights back when meddled with, and is a forceful opponent.

Calico always thought of her father as steel-strong and flint-hard, but kind and gentle as well, until she discovered he had drowned a litter of kittens. Her father realised how upset she was about it, Calico thought he never killed anything else after that incident, but he still went on killing foxes, rabbits, moles, interbred kittens and puppies; he just never let her find out. It was part of nature. Living and working alongside and with nature he had become an extension of it, conscience, the rights and wrongs of killing, did not enter into it. The foxes killed his poultry; the rabbits brought disease and ate his grass; the moles heaped up the soil; the litters of young were too interbred, better off dead than disabled animals breeding more unfortunate offspring, so he destroyed them. Nature has a cruel side, she gave cats their evil streak, the pleasure they take in torturing their prey. At least man, if he is humane, gives his victim a quick clean death. Calico's father never used metal traps for catching vermin, ironically he thought they caused too much suffering to the animal.

It was difficult for Calico to understand her father's attitude. It seemed to be a case of protecting your own; anything that interfered with that was disposed of forthwith, thus allowing wild animals a free run of the place, until they abused this privilege. If one of his poultry died of natural causes, Calico's father would leave it at the bottom of the parrock for the fox to eat. But woe betide that fox if he dared to attack his live poultry, he would be hunted down and killed without remorse. A sort of live and let live to a certain extent. He also did not welcome the interference of others doing his killing for him, especially if the animal suffered in the process. The hunt he would not allow on his land. A long time ago he had purchased an old American jeep in a farm sale. He would race after them in this noisy contraption if he sighted them on his land, saving many a fox from a nasty fate.

Calico knew she would never make a farmer, the place would go to pieces. She would let the foxes live whatever they did; she would want to keep all the calves, instead of selecting a few and sending the rest to market; she would not kill the poultry that had been fattened up for Christmas. She would be hopeless. She did not have whatever it takes to be a farmer, or for that matter a farmer's wife. She cringed at the thought of chopping the head off a chicken, plucking it and gutting it; or skinning a rabbit; or preparing rooks or pigeons for a pie. it was not so long ago that most wives were expected to know how to prepare poultry, game and fish from its natural state, bought from the local poacher, farmer, or market stall. No prepared, jointed, and shrink-wrapped supermarket packages then.

In the hay-making field Calico rested on the stack of bales she had just put up. The baler had broken down yet again, and her father had his nose in its insides, tinkering about and trying to sort the problem out. He was not very pleased. The baler had two fuel tanks, one for t.v.o. the other for petrol. The baler's engine started up on petrol and was then turned over to t.v.o., which was cheaper being for agricultural use. Every end of summer, after hay-making, he drained the petrol from the tank (because it would evaporate), to protect the tank from rusting, filled it up with t.v.o. for the winter. This summer when he came to drain the t.v.o. out of the petrol tank, the tank was empty. He refilled it with petrol and could find no leaks. Talking it over with his wife he remembered that in the winter, Barney from the local council houses had trouble with his car. He was pushing it down the road. When the car eventually started, clouds of dark grey smoke flew out from under the backend, and it smelt of t.v.o. So putting two and two together he realised what must have happened. *Serve the bugger right*, he thought, *that'll larn 'im*. He had never locked up anything until Barney came to live in the village and things started disappearing. Calico was grateful for the breather the baler gave her. The sky was bright blue and cloudless. She shut her eyes against the glare of the sun. Her mother was turning the hay in the next field, driving the old two-seater David Brown tractor, with the Vicon Leyly hitched up to it. Calico could hear the tractor engine being shut down to negotiate the corners, and opened up again for the straights. The sweet scent of flowering honeysuckle drifted across her nostrils. The sound of the bees buzzing busily as they made their collections from it. Then another noise assaulted her ear drums. 'Damn,' she swore out loud. 'He's got the baler working.'

Calico slid down from her peaceful perch, and started walking towards the place the next seven bales would be dropped. Leonie, who had been lying in the shade of the hedge, joined her mistress. Liaka was confined to the house. Her mating had been successful and her puppies had been due to arrive four days ago. Calico had taken her to the vet that morning, because she was worried about her and thought something might be wrong. Liaka was huge, it looked as though she carried a large litter. Calico had read that German Shepherd bitches usually whelped a few days early, and the bigger the litter the earlier they whelped. If that was the case she was more than four days over her time. The vet had told her it was nothing to worry about, bitches were often as much as a couple of weeks overdue, she looked healthy enough in herself. He estimated nine to twelve puppies were inside, after he had felt around internally. He gave her a calcium injection, as she was panting a little too fast, and told Calico to bring her in again in a couple of days, if there was still no sign of the puppies.

Calico's mother and father had to break from the hay-making to do the milking. That meant Calico had a couple of hours respite; then they all rushed back out to the fields. Calico and her mother took out the tractor with the front loader attached and her father followed in the old lorry, to get a few loads of bales into the barn before darkness fell. Calico liked riding on the top of the last load home. Lying back she would watch the sky as it darkened and the stars appeared, feeling the gentle swaying of the bales beneath her. It could be dangerous, more than once the load had collapsed on the journey.

No one seemed to worry about this. Ever since she was a small child Calico had been riding in on the loads, shinning up the ladder to the top of the barn, standing on the bales around the edge; it all had seemed quite natural to her. Like riding on the backs of the quieter cows, and driving the tractors.

Calico took Liaka's temperature before she went to bed that evening, to find out if the puppies were imminent. But her temperature had not dropped at all, so it was not worth Calico staying up with her all night. The next morning when Calico came downstairs, she noticed the newspaper in the whelping box had a green stain on it. She checked

Liaka and found she had a slight green discharge. Calico telephoned the vet.

'Good,' he said. 'That's what I wanted to hear. The puppies will be coming soon.'

By lunchtime no puppies had arrived. Her father thought there may be a dead puppy inside, because the green colouring was from the placenta. Dealing with numerous births over the years, he told her that Liaka should have started whelping by now, and to take her into the vet's surgery. Calico rang the vet again.

'Take her for a walk,' the vet advised. 'that will probably get them moving.'

'Take her to the vet. It's no good him handing out advice over the phone. There's something not right there.' said her father.

The vet did not seem very pleased to see Calico. He put on his surgical gloves, examined Liaka internally, and gave her an injection, 'To give her a hint to get started,' he said, and that was it. The green discharge was now more profuse. Calico stayed with Liaka all night expecting her to give birth at any minute. It was not until the next morning that Liaka started tearing up the paper in her whelping box. Calico gave her some warm milk, glucose, and an egg mixed together, to help her with the ordeal ahead. She lapped it up, turned round, and promptly brought it all back up again. She laid down. Calico cleared up the mess. 'Mum, Dad, quick,' she shouted. 'The contractions have started.'

Calico was so pleased, all that waiting and worrying, but it had been worth it now the puppies were on their way.

'Here it comes, the first one,' she said proudly, hardly able to contain her excitement. 'No 'tisn't,' corrected her father. ''Tis the water bag that comes fust, as a buffer.' Liaka stood up, the puppy left her with a dull thud. Nobody moved for a moment. 'It's a pup!' exclaimed Calico. 'There's no water bag.'

'That's mighty peculiar,' replied her father. Liaka stood looking at the deposit she had made. Then she licked vigorously at the membrane surrounding the puppy. Feeling no response, she tried to bury it under the newspapers in her box.

'Oh no! Quick give it to me. I'll try to revive it,' said Calico's mother urgently.

Calico handed her the perfectly formed, little lifeless body, covered in slime-green placenta. 'It's no good,' her mother said despairingly. 'It's been dead a while. Liaka must have realised. That's why she tried to dispose of it. Sometimes they eat it.'

Calico looked at her sadly. The next puppy came out without its placenta, also dead. The poor bitch, not understanding what was wrong with it, bit right through to the bone of its leg trying to get a response from it. 'The third one must be all right,' wailed Calico. 'Ring the vet,' insisted Calico's father. 'Like I been saying all along, there's something not right here.'

The vet came. He gave Liaka an injection to slow down the contractions. He told them that being a maiden bitch she was trying to hurry things along, to get it over with as soon as possible. She was giving birth too quickly and the placenta was being left behind each time. 'Ring me after the next puppy appears, even if it's all right. I'd like to know,' he said on his way out.

The third pup had no placenta and was dead on arrival. Calico was nearly in tears. They were so well-formed. Shiny black coats, as if they had been polished for the occasion. Little pink ears and little pink paws.

She could visualise each one as a fully grown dog. She would have understood if they had been malformed, maybe better off dead in that case. But not these. These were perfect. She rang the vet. 'Bring her in for a Caesarean,' his receptionist told her.

'Will she be all right,' asked Calico.

'At least you will have some puppies,' she answered. Calico left Liaka in the hands of the vet. 'We'll ring you as soon as we have any news,' he informed her.

Calico felt better on the way home. She was disappointed when the first three puppies had been born dead. Now there was still something to look forward to at least. She wondered how many puppies would be coming home with Liaka tomorrow. Maybe six to nine, according to the vet's previous estimation of the litter number. Liaka had eight teats giving milk. Twelve puppies would have put a tremendous strain on her. Perhaps it was just as well a few fell by the wayside. Calico consoled herself with thoughts along these lines. Trying to make out whatever happens is for the best, and there is a reason for the tragedies that befall us.

Calico's mother and father came in from the fields to have a cup of tea, and a piece of cake, before milking. They had been mowing, so Calico had not been needed that afternoon. 'How many?' inquired Calico's mother, as soon as she entered the kitchen.

'No news yet, Mum. I would have rushed out to tell you, if there had been,' replied Calico. Her father came into the kitchen as she was saying this, and as if on cue, the telephone rang. Calico smiled, relieved. 'How many do you say?' she asked her parents.

'Seven,' answered her father.

'Six,' said her mother.

'I'll say eight, fingers crossed,' Calico said as she went into the hall to answer the telephone. Calico re-entered the kitchen slowly. Her parents looked at her expectantly.

'They are all dead,' she informed them, her voice breaking up. And then she burst into uncontrollable sobbing, the tears flooding down her face. She tried to tell her parents what the vet had said, but she was incoherent for a while.

'What Liaka as well?' questioned her mother, biting her lip and blinking hard to stop herself from crying.

'No, no,' Calico managed to say between sobs.

Her father got up quickly from his chair. 'I'll go and tie the cows up Mother,' he said abruptly. He could not sit and watch his daughter weeping as if her heart was irretrievably broken. He could not bear it. He felt like crying alongside her; she looked such a heart-rending sight. But that would never do, men do not cry, they have to be emotionally strong. Crying is a sign of weakness. So instead of staying and comforting Calico when she needed him, he walked away.

'Why does God do it, Mum?' questioned Calico. 'Why does he give us such heartache? What had those little puppies done that he took their chance of life away? The vet said there was nothing wrong with them. Seven, all perfectly formed. He could not understand it. Two of them had heartbeats, but he could not revive them. He said there was no reason for it, they should have been all right. Why did they die?' Now Calico had started talking she could not stop herself gabbling on.

'Poor Liaka, carrying them around for all those weeks. Giving them the calcium, vitamins, minerals, and proteins from her own body; so they would have a good start in life. Making all that milk ready for their nourishment. Taking them full term, and then losing every one of them. Not one out of ten surviving. All that effort, the pain of the operation and nothing to show for it.'

'It is difficult to understand,' replied Calico's mother, when Calico finally stopped for breath. 'But there is nothing we can do about it. There is something greater than us that decides these things. You have to put it behind you, not dwell on it, look to the future. You have one consolation, Liaka survived. Imagine how much worse you would be feeling if she had gone as well.'

'Your trouble, Mother,' retorted Calico, 'is that you are too sensible, and don't indulge in self-pity. Some people spend their whole life indulging in self-pity. You won't even allow me half an hour of it before you begin telling me to pull myself together, and count the blessings I have left. It's my own fault I suppose for imagining what the puppies would be like. Wondering if any of them would be show winners. It was to be the start of my own strain. These puppies would have been the first under the Jaquenetta kennel name. You're right I'm crying for myself, for my own disappointment, as well as for Liaka and her ten dead off-spring. That's what happens when you build a castle in the air. A jet plane called "reality" goes screaming through and knocks it to pieces, that come crashing down around you. Your dreams fall as rubble at your feet.'

One effect this tragedy had on Calico was to change her attitude towards the adult world of the Mansion House. It is odd how tragedy turns our brain slightly, allows us to step outside of our normal character, to do things we would not usually do; it changes the way we think for a while and gives us a reckless licence. We question if there is a God. We either turn to Him and become closer to Him, or we think He must have forsaken us. We feel the need to fight against Him, to do an action which would not meet with His approval. This defiance was in Calico's mind when she decided to accept Charles's advances, and go out with him the next time he asked her. *My piece of patchwork has only just begun in this my growing-up year. I have done nothing that warranted colour in my life before this*, thought Calico. She was looking forward to returning to the Mansion House, and what it held in store for her.

Chapter Seven

An Invitation into Society

Society is now one polish'd horde,
Form'd of two mighty tribes, the bores and bored.

Byron

Several months after that first apprehensive journey towards a different way of life, Calico was once again travelling the same route. This time she was more confident; this time she knew what to expect.

On arrival at the Mansion House, Calico endured the usual taunts about having the two hottest weeks of the year off, and coming back without the merest tinge of a suntan. Amy was pleased to see her ally again. Mr Rolph and Sophia were still peeved about the incident with the starch. They were watching Amy closely, hoping to get even with her. Now Calico had returned, they had her to concentrate on as well thereby taking some of the pressure off Amy.

The conversations around the kitchen table seemed unaltered by her absence. Grace was still making excuses for her bully of a husband. Vera was still worrying about her mother's health. Maria had yet another appointment at the infertility clinic. The cook and Susan were still arguing over Royalty. Susan, believing all people are equal, and that the Royal Family were only in their position by fortunate births, resented the country subsidising them, when she felt there were better causes to spend the money on. 'They're living off the state. No different than the people on the dole,' she said, 'except they get a much bigger giro cheque than most, and have greater assets.'

The cook would get most upset, but however much she tried to defend them, Susan would always have an answer against them. Often breaktimes ended early, as Cook, thoroughly exasperated by coming up against a brick wall of argument, would be determined to have the last word. She would call end of break immediately after it, before Susan could retaliate. It was the only way Cook could get the better of her. To avoid this happening all the others present would butt in and try to change the subject; whenever a confrontation seemed imminent.

There was one difference Calico noticed on her return, and that was the way Tryphena treated her. She actually sought out Calico, going out of her way to be friendly, asking Calico to her room for coffee and chats. Even, much to Calico's surprise, inviting her to accompany her to a party. Calico refused with various excuses, all of which Tryphena parried.

'I won't know anyone.'

'You'll know me.'

'I won't know what to talk about.'

'You know about lots of things.'

'I haven't anything suitable to wear.'

'You can borrow something of mine.'

And so on, until Calico gave in and agreed to go.

Calico was nervous the evening she got ready for the party. She asked Amy to do her face and hair. Amy did not seem to mind that she had been left out of the invitation. She did not think she would have enjoyed herself. Calico was inclined to agree with her. Neither had much time to spare for the shallow social set. Calico was not used to people who did not say what they meant, and were overfriendly to everyone with money or influence that might be of use to them in their upwardly mobile progress. And Amy had met too many of them through her mother. Amy told Calico about their empty promises to secure contacts to further their ambitions. Many times her mother had introduced a person to the social scene, only to find herself being snubbed by that same person, after they had used her contacts as stepping stones to get what they wanted. Amy had seen the hurt look in her mother's eyes, as the realisation dawned that she had been used yet again, and this time, as always, she thought they were different. Her mother, desperate to know the 'right people', did not have the ruthless streak needed to make use of them. She went to parties nearly every night, leaving little Amy with anyone who would look after her. Amy could remember a succession of men filtering through her young life. None stayed around long. Her mother spent her life searching for an elusive happiness, never content with her present life, always wanting more. She was on the fringe of the social scene, observing the central people who had 'made it', wanting to be there with them. Striving towards that position, making every effort to be accepted into the revered circle, but always being in their eyes sideline material. Consequently Amy was neglected, not physically, she was always fed and well-clothed; but emotionally. She grew up desperate for a show of affection. Boys were attracted to her in her early teens, largely due to her well-developed bust. She started being intimate with them at quite an early age, mistaking lust and lover's oaths in the heat of the moment, for love and affection. She did not enjoy the act of making love, but the intimacy that accompanied it. What she enjoyed was the feel of somebody really close to her, of somebody wanting her, and being cuddled and held in someone's arms. Having someone there all to herself. Being the centre of their undivided attention. Starved of love and outward signs of affection for so many years, Amy fell ravenously upon this source indulging herself gluttonously for a while. Until she realised that it was not a substitute for love, it meant little to the other party, and they seldom stayed with her for long. She became more selective after that, paced herself accordingly, and did not sleep with a boy on their first meeting. Which meant a lot of them failed to turn up for the second, the reputation having preceded her of being an 'easy lay', when the rumour proved untrue, they felt cheated.

Amy decided the social set was responsible for her unhappy childhood. She did not blame her mother's yearnings. It is difficult to find fault with those we love, it is far easier to shift the blame to unknown faces. In Amy's mind the fault lay with the social set's treatment of her mother, so Amy despised them.

Tryphena drove them to the party venue in her latest acquisition which was bright red, long, low, sleek, and squealed around corners. Calico, being used to plodding up hill and down dale at a steady forty miles an hour in an old farm truck, did not find the journey very pleasant. Alongside her father, the countryside ambled by, in this contraption it flashed. Father in his old truck, would spend more time with his eyes on the state of the grass and the livestock in the fields of other farmers, than on the road he was travelling. *Thank heavens Tryphena does not do the same at this speed*, thought Calico.

Tryphena aimed the car between a pair of ornate wrought-iron gates, and up a tree-lined drive. They came to an abrupt halt with a spray of gravel, in front of a huge country house, which in comparison made the Mansion House seem no bigger than a farmworker's cottage. Tryphena had already warned Calico not to say where they worked or what they did for a living. She had told this particular social circle that she was at university, and advised Calico to say the same. This accounted for the opening remark from the hostess, 'Oh super, you made it. Not bogged down frightfully with studying then? You intellectuals, always seem to have your nose in a book, while the social whirl passes you by.'

Calico looked at Tryphena, but Tryphena would not return the glance. 'We do come up for air sometimes you know,' trilled Tryphena. 'It's not all dusty tomes and ink-stained fingers.'

'Come and meet the others,' insisted the hostess. 'You may know some of the younger ones, they're at varsity too.'

'Now what do we do?' hissed Calico to Tryphena, as they obediently followed her.

'Stop worrying. This lot are bound to attend either Oxford or Cambridge, with their money and connections,' Tryphena reassured her. 'So we can mention any local one quite safely.'

Calico was still not convinced she would be able to go through with this pretence.

'What do you tell them you're studying, when they ask?' queried Calico.

'You have to get in first, ask what they are reading for, and then you can choose a different subject,' confided Tryphena. She made it sound so easy, but then she had been living this way for years. The lies tripped off her tongue, combined with her charm and her haughty elegance, and she captivated her audience who never saw reason to question her breeding or her way of life. The evidence was before them in the way she spoke; the way she dressed; the cars she drove; the places she had been; the people she knew; everything about her – the complete outward façade, which marked her in the same category as they put themselves.

It was ironic that Tryphena, a fallen woman, was accepted into the social scene, whilst Amy's mother never had been. Which proved to Calico that outward show was what counted with these sort of people. To look as though you had plenty of money, was more important than a quick wit or an entertaining personality. No price could be put on these attributes, so to this class of society they were valueless.

Calico sat quietly listening to these people. There was no problem hearing them. They all talked in loud carrying tones, as if addressing an audience from centre stage. The group nearest to her had discovered a common bond: they all owned a villa in France. They were discussing all the advantages that went with it, how clever they were to invest in foreign properties, while they were such a snip of a price; how marvellous to be able to pop over to it for every holiday. Calico thought it would have made more sense, if each had bought a villa in a different country. Then they could have travelled around Europe, instead of visiting the same place year after year.

Another group discussed works of art, and the ones they had purchased recently. One woman considered herself a patron of the arts, because several times a year she flew across to Paris and visited the artists' quarter. She would select original oil paintings from the artists, who exhibited their work at the Place du Tertre. She did not hang the paintings, as not being famous names yet they would not impress people. She stored them all in the attic, keeping a note of the names in case one of them became known. Then she could proudly display her painting as their early work, saying she had spotted their talent straight away.

Calico knew about Montmartre, where the Place du Tertre was situated. She had read about all the places she overheard in their conversations from old guide books that her father had bought at a farm sale. He had wanted a wall clock and the books had been in the same lot number. Calico had devoured them, imagined herself there. These people visited them regularly in the fashionable style and when they were in season.

In Florence their hotel rooms had to overlook the River Arno and the Ponte Vecchio. In Rome the Via Veneto was the street to stay at, and the Caffe Greco the place to go for atmosphere. Venice had to be visited at carnival time, staying at the hotel next to the Doge's Palace. Every year La Scala in Milan had to be attended, whether they enjoyed opera or not was irrelevant. This was the only thing Calico envied about these people, the places they had seen, but not the way in which they seen them. Not wandering off the expensive path mapped out for them to catch the colourful character of the country.

Calico saw their shallow smiles, heard the hollow laughter echo on their lips. They did not seem like real people to her, more like surface creations with reflected opinions; not of the outside world, but of a self-created world: protected, cocooned, and cosseted by wealth and position. They talked at, not with, each other, about the latest impressive acquisition, the profit they made last year, the hectic social life they led.

Calico was relieved when Tryphena said it was time to leave. She had nothing in common with these people. What amazed her concerning them was the way they followed trends. She could understand why creative people crept around them. They had the power to make or break an artist or writer, whether a genius or not. If one of these people took them up as their pet project, their discovery, all the other gullibles followed suit, and he or she was 'in'. The same with fashion designers. Once 'in' high prices could be commanded, for work one of the villagers back home could probably do just as well. It was sad to see the hypocrisy among these people. It reminded her of a play she had read,

The Revenger's Tragedy by Tourneur, the imagery of masks featuring as a recurring theme, the painted faces and fine clothes of the outward appearance masking the evil within. People taken by their surface value, their face mask, but the skull is lurking just beneath, showing death ever present.

To be fair to these people, they probably did not realise the way they acted, never stopped to consider what they did. As everyone else in their set was like-minded, it would seem the normal way to live. Whether they really enjoyed life, they did not doubt, of course everything was absolutely super.

Calico sat quite still with her fingers crossed on the journey back. Bracing herself ready for an accident. Fortunately most other people must have had a foreboding about Tryphena's driving. They only met a couple of cars that had ventured out, and now fervently wished they had not. Calico got out of the car, grateful to be back on her own two feet, still in one piece. Tryphena went to the front steps. She was allowed to use this door, and had been given a key for it.

'You coming in this way?' she asked Calico.

'No, I'd better not. I'll use the staff entrance, I've got my key to that. Thanks for taking me. Goodnight,' answered Calico warily.

'All right, if you're worried about being seen. Goodnight,' replied Tryphena.

Calico made her way around to the other door. It was rather dark as the streetlights were out. She had reached the door, when she heard a noise behind her. Someone grabbed her, well it was more of a fumble, and a voice said close to her ear. 'Don't scream Calico, it's me Charles.' He turned her round. By the moon's faint light she could make out his outline. He bent his head towards her, tightened his hold on her, and kissed her.

It was an odd sensation being kissed surrounded by darkness. It heightened the feeling of the lips and the bodies touching, concentrated by the absence of sight. She submerged herself in the feel of him, his lips, his tongue, his teeth, the nearness of him pressing against her. Then she panicked. He held her more closely, as if trying to absorb her into him. She felt something hard against her belly, she felt him trembling. She could not cope with this, it was new to her. She felt suffocated by it, frightened by the intensity of him: his panting breath; his lips all over her face, her neck, in her hair. She tried to break away. 'Charles, please,' she said quietly. 'I'm not ready for this.'

'Sorry,' apologised Charles. 'I got carried away. I want you so much, I find it hard to control myself.' Charles was, for once, speaking the truth. He was so used to going out with willing women, that he found it difficult to slow down his pace. He did not have to worry about rushing the majority of his conquests. They knew as much about sex as he did, and would have been most put out if he had not tried to make love to them as soon as they met. With Calico it was different, she was a challenge. She transported him back to the courting days of his youth and made him use his art of seduction to the full. It was not unpleasant, the agony, the tortured feelings, the excitement of the chase. Charles relaxed his grip on Calico. She moved back half a step, relieved. 'I've been waiting here ages for you,' whispered Charles. 'I've been trying to see you alone ever since you returned from your holiday. You know how I feel about you. Please let me see you, let me spend some time in your company. Just let me be with you for a while. Please.'

'I don't know,' hesitated Calico, uncertain.

'Please, please just once. Let me take you out once at least. Give me that chance of happiness, to have you to myself, even if only for a few hours. I can't stop thinking about you. Let me have one night to remember,' pleaded

Charles. 'You looked so breathtakingly beautiful tonight. I saw you leave with Tryphena. I had to come back to see you. I couldn't help myself. See what you've done to me, I'm not responsible for my own actions. You've captivated me. Put me out of my misery, say yes, please.'

'Oh all right!' exclaimed Calico. 'If only to stop you wittering on and on.'

Charles pressed her tightly to him for a few seconds. 'Thanks. Oh God, thanks,' he murmured, with his eyes closed as if offering up a prayer.

Calico felt strange to be the producer of so much emotion in another being. Having Charles begging her to spend some time with him as if it was crucial to his existence that she say yes. How could she refuse? It obviously meant a great deal to him. It would not hurt to see him just the once.

'Thursday okay. I'll pick you up about seven thirty,' said Charles, not wasting any time now he had gained the answer he wanted.

'I thought you were working Thursday. The Lord Mayor's got an evening do at the Council House,' she retorted.

'I am,' replied Charles. 'I'll take her to her do at seven o'clock. You wait for me at the top of the road. I'll come back in the car and pick you up.'

'In the Daimler?' Calico said dubiously.

'Yes. It'll be all right. People round here are used to seeing it,' assured Charles.

Calico opened her mouth to protest. Charles cut in quickly. 'I'll see you Thursday night. Calico, you don't realise how much this means to me.' He kissed her, clung to her for a moment, then disappeared into the darkness.

Calico unlocked the door, and went straight up to her bedroom, with feelings and sensations, thoughts and dreams, all mingling together in her, and a deep uncertainty and dread in the pit of her stomach over what lay ahead.

Chapter Eight

The Passionate Versus the Prudish

> Strong as our passions are, they may be starved into submission, and conquered without being killed.
>
> Colton

Brydle was twinned with a city of similar size in France. The French dignitaries had enjoyed the hospitality of Brydle and it was now their turn to reciprocate. This was good news to the staff. It meant they would have a free weekend, while the Lord Mayor and her consort were absent.

During the week previous to their trip, the Lord Mayor spent most of her time buying clothes, and then having them altered. The gardener's wife, who had been given the position of personal laundress-cum-maid to the Mayor, was asked to attend full-time for this week. The Lord Mayor flitted in and out at odd times, so Cook was not required to prepare lunch, only to cater for the staff. The Mayor and her husband being Jews, pork was seldom on the menu for the staff; today it was.

Calico happened to be in the kitchen when the Cook removed the joint of pork from the oven. The rind was a crisp golden brown. Suddenly the Lord Mayor appeared. Cook reacted like a startled hare. The Lord Mayor attacked the joint of pork, tearing off chunks of crackling and cramming them into her mouth. Liquid fat oozing out at the corners, and trickling down her chin. Her fingers were covered with grease. Painted blood-red fingernails clawing into the flesh, transferring it in lumps to her smeary blood-red lips. Calico stood transfixed at the spectacle. It reminded her of a bird with its prey; she did have a passing resemblance to a vulture with that nose, and those beady eyes.

'Have you a napkin I can use Cook?' asked the Lord Mayor, when she had finished mutilating the pork joint. Cook, without a word, handed her a napkin.

'I cannot resist pork crackling. The aroma wafted up to me as I entered the front door, sheer torture to the senses,' she said, as she wiped her hands and lips. Leaving a red stain on the white linen.

'Well!' exclaimed Cook when the Lord Mayor had departed. 'What do you make of that?'

Calico shook her head, unable to give an answer.

'It must be right, what I heard about her,' continued the Cook. 'They say she isn't a Jew by birth, but has put on an act for years. Her husband stands to inherit a lot of money from his older brother in America. It's the family fortune left to him by the parents. If the brother knew she wasn't a Jew, he would leave the money to someone else. I also heard that she had an affair with the brother and that's why he went to live in America.'

More intrigue, thought Calico. So they both led a double life. Obviously the Lord Mayor knew about the consort's afternoon assignations, tolerating them because she was not without blemishes herself, and looking towards the inheritance dangling in front of them.

Calico did not tell Amy she was meeting the chauffeur, she could not bring herself to admit the fact to another person. She did not realise it was guilt that prevented her from imparting the information, but her subconscious did. That part of her knew what she was doing was wrong and against God's teachings, meeting a married man. But her other self, the one that puts us forward to get knocked down, that is battered and bruised by the blows life deals out and picks us up and puts us back in the ring again, as if we have not suffered enough, was waiting at the top of the road before seven thirty for Charles to appear.

Charles could not refrain from looking like a happy moron, ever since Calico had agreed to meet him. He was so pleased with himself. Every time he thought about it he began effervescing inside, erupting into an idiotic grin. From the moment he had fixed the date with Calico, time seemed to slow down and hang suspended. He could not believe it was only a few days ago. Time seems to relate itself to whether we are looking forward to or dreading, an event, and paces itself accordingly to cause the most consternation. His impatience with time also affected his driving, making him drive faster, as if by doing so he could hurry time along. Tonight especially, when he took the Lord Mayor to the Council House at seven o'clock, he drove rather fast, which did not go unnoticed: 'Are we in a hurry?' questioned the Lord Mayor sardonically.

'No, but I am,' quipped Charles.

All sorts of reactions went on inside Charles as his eyes focused on Calico. He saw the figure in a long purple dress as soon as he reached the brow of the hill. He drove down towards her, slowly now. The feelings within him, the surge of adrenalin mixing up his emotions; he needed time to bring them all under control before he faced her. The effect she had on him, while being exciting, was not good for his ego.

He stopped the car in front of her. She opened the passenger door to sit next to him.

'Sit in the back and see what it's like to be a celebrity. Wave at the people,' he suggested to her, getting out and going around to her side. He opened the door for her. 'Your carriage awaits, Madam.' She smiled at him and entered the back of the car.

'I could set up house in here,' she said, amazed at all the space. There was room for six people to travel comfortably. The seats were upholstered in black leather, a plush maroon carpet covered the floor with maroon velvet curtains at the windows, held back with gold braided tassels. This was travelling in style. The people they passed on the pavements all turned their heads to watch them glide by. She could not hear the engine, or feel the unevenness of the road being cushioned inside. She wondered if her father ever dreamt of owning a car like this, but then he would probably take the calves to market in the back, or turn it into a chicken house. He did not have much time for 'fancy' items, believing everything should have a use, and be able to do the job it was intended for, without a lot of superfluous paraphernalia attached to it.

The car came to a halt opposite a public house. Charles got out of the driver's seat, came round to the nearside of the car, and opened the door for Calico. 'You wait for me here. I'll go and park the car in its allocated space, in front of the Council House, just around the corner. I won't be long.' Calico obediently vacated the back seat. She watched the car until it disappeared out of her sight. She turned and gazed, without focusing her eyes on anything in particular, into the shop window immediately in front of her. *It's not too late to do a runner*, thought Calico, but her feet remained immobile. She was uncertain about what she was doing there, she still had misgivings. Before she could sort out her thoughts, Charles appeared at her side. All else was forgotten as her body responded to the sight of him and took over the control of her actions.

Charles took hold of her arm and propelled her across the road. He opened the door of the public house, and stood back to allow her to enter. 'Thank you,' said Calico politely.

'What would you like to drink?' asked Charles.

Calico was not familiar with the drinks people chose in pubs. The only drink she liked that was slightly alcoholic was Babycham, so she asked for that.

'That's not much of a drink,' scoffed Charles, 'unless you have brandy with it.'

'I don't know whether I'd like that,' she replied.

'If you don't, I'll drink it and get you something else,' he assured her.

Charles got their drinks and shepherded her into a corner seat. Calico took a tentative sip of her drink. It tasted quite nice. 'Is it okay?' said Charles indicating her drink.

'Fine, thank you,' she answered, looking round at the other customers. The men all looked vaguely similar in attire, and were looking her way.

'Charles. Are most of these chauffeurs?' she queried.

'Yes,' he replied. 'When there's a big do on at the Council House, the chauffeurs congregate in here.'

'Do they know you?'

'Most of them.'

Calico fell silent. This is not what she had expected, to be the centre of probing eyes and knowing smiles. Her cheeks were burning under their gazes. She felt the colour flooding into her cheeks. She must look (as her gran would have put it) red enough to lay.

'Charles can we leave?' urged Calico.

'Sorry. I can't leave here,' he said, apologetically. 'The Lord Mayor's secretary telephones this pub just before the do is over, so we're ready and waiting when it finishes.'

Calico felt most uncomfortable and wished herself miles away from here. What must the other chauffeurs think of her? How could Charles be so insensitive as to bring her to this place, or was he pandering to his ego? *I cannot endure this*, she thought, *I've got to get out of here*.

'Charles, take me back,' she demanded suddenly.

'I can't,' he protested. 'I can't take you back to the Mansion House yet.'

'Please Charles. I can't stay here,' she pleaded. 'Not with all these people you know.'

'Don't take any notice of them,' laughed Charles. 'Is that why you want to leave?'

'Yes. Don't make me stay Charles, please,' she implored, looking dolefully at him.

'Okay, I'll ring for a taxi,' he said impatiently.

'Thanks,' she said gratefully, letting a sigh escape.

'You will come out with me again?' he questioned, wanting to make sure he was going to get another chance to see her, before he let her leave so easily.

'I don't know,' she answered truthfully.

'Please. I won't bring you here. I didn't realise it would upset you,' he said, seemingly concerned. 'We'll go to another pub, and I'll leave the telephone number with the secretary, so he can call me there.'

'All right,' said Calico reluctantly, knowing that the sooner she agreed, the quicker she would be able to leave. Charles had got the answer he desired and went to telephone for a taxi. Calico felt even more like a shop window display now she was left on her own. She gulped down the rest of her drink. Charles beckoned to her. She went across to him. He steered her through a side door, that led out into a dimly lit alley.

'That was quick!' exclaimed Calico. 'I was expecting to have to wait awhile.'

'The taxi isn't here yet. I thought you'd rather wait outside for it to arrive,' Charles informed her. In fact he had not booked the taxi to arrive for another half an hour, but he was not going to tell Calico that.

Calico shivered out here in the chilly darkness, after the warmth of the pub.

'Here,' said Charles, removing his jacket and putting it round her shoulders. 'You're cold. Let's slip into the shadows of this shop doorway to keep warm.' He gently persuaded her to him. She snuggled into his body seeking warmth.

'I wish you'd stay,' Charles murmured. Calico did not comment. 'Can I see you over the weekend, when the Lord Mayor's away?' continued Charles.

'Sorry, I'm going home this weekend,' answered Calico.

'I can't wait until next week. The last few days have dragged on like a year. It'll seem like another two if I have to wait until next week.' said Charles mournfully. He was getting worried now, he seemed to be losing her interest. She obviously did not feel the same way about him, as he did about her.

'I've made arrangements now. The family will be expecting me,' she replied firmly.

'Monday evening then,' persisted Charles. He sounded so despairing, Calico finally agreed to another meeting. They stood kissing and caressing for a while, lost in each other, until the sound of a car horn parted them. Calico's taxi had arrived. Charles gave the driver enough money to cover the fare, and went back into the pub amidst nudges and winks directed at him by the other chauffeurs, interspersed with lewd smiles and crude comments.

The evening had disappointed Calico so she preferred to put it out of her mind and concentrate on looking forward to going home for a long weekend. The Lord Mayor and all the 'hangers-on', breakfasted early, before catching the plane to take them to France. The staff had to work for a few more hours, so as to leave the place clean and tidy. Calico and Amy caught the bus into the city centre and browsed round the shops, then went their respective ways. Amy towards the café where she had arranged to meet John, and Calico towards the bus depot to catch her bus home.

On the way to the bus station Calico heard a car horn hooting, and someone shouting her name. She turned around expecting to see Charles.

'Hello Calico, it is you. I hoped it was. I wasn't too sure, I recognised the patchwork inserts,' said the driver of a large black saloon car.

'William,' was all Calico managed to say.

'Can I give you a lift back to work?' he ventured.

'No,' answered Calico. William's smile faded. 'But I wouldn't mind a lift home.'

His face brightened, 'That's great, hop in,' he said pleased at this opportunity.

'What are you doing in the big city?' Calico asked when she was seated next to him.

'I've been to the maternity hospital,' he replied.

'Oh!' Calico did not like to enquire further.

'My sister's had a baby, and I've been visiting her and my new nephew,' he explained.

They chatted amicably most of the journey. As directed by Calico, he drove into the farm courtyard, spraying chicken and geese all ways. Calico was greeted effusively by Leonie and Liaka, who had made a full recovery after her ordeal. William was spotted by Calico's mother. She insisted he joined them for a cup of tea and a piece of cake. William got on well with Calico's parents, having so much in common to talk about. Her father suggested she show William around the farm. Calico obliged. They finished up at the outhouses, to see the calves her father was bringing on: the little white-faced Hereford bull calf called Barnaby, already with headbutting tendencies; the boney little Ayrshires with charred buds where a set of horns, upstanding as a reindeer's, should have been starting to grow, were named Jayne, Marilyn, and Diana, because Calico's father hoped their udders would follow their namesakes in size, and they would grow into good milkers. There were also some sturdy Friesians and shorthorns; a pure white curly-coated calf named Fiona, and a blue-roan called Charlotte.

All the farm animals were known by name, often earning their name by their own actions. One cow was nicknamed 'Tear-ass', as she was constantly catching her behind on barbwire fences; her official name was Penelope. Flower names like buttercup and daisy had given way to topical names like Apollo, Splashdown and Concorde; or names in the news like Christine and Mandy.

'You'll have to come and see our farm,' suggested William. 'Why don't I come and pick you up tomorrow evening after milking? I'll show you around the farm, and perhaps we could stop for a drink on the way home.'

'Yes, all right,' said Calico. It would be nice, she thought, he was pleasant. Not silver-tongued and sensual like Charles. William did not excite her body as she stood close to him. She felt at ease with him, in control of her feelings. She did not know that William wanted to take her in his arms and kiss her, but he had respect for women as equal beings, and more self-control in his little finger than Charles had over his whole body.

'This farmhouse is very old isn't it?' William observed, making conversation again.

'Some parts are fourteenth-century. They do say that Judge Jeffries held court here. There are several cells inside with barred windows. There's a room at the back with stone steps leading up to it, and they dip in the middle from wear. Running away from the bottom of these stone steps is a dead end passage, it seems to be between the kitchen and the dining room. The house used to be three storeys high. There was a fire in the top storey and it was never rebuilt, they just re-roofed the lower two storeys,' Calico rambled on. She loved this old house and its history.

William reluctantly took his leave of Calico. He arranged to pick her up at six o'clock the next evening. After he had gone, Calico leant over the wooden gate surveying the fields, watching a couple of rabbits darting about quite near to her. Liaka, who had been sat quietly at the feet of her mistress, could contain herself no longer. She cleared the wall and bounded towards the rabbits, scattering them in all directions. Leonie, seeing that Liaka was not reprimanded for her behaviour, followed suit. Calico climbed over the gate at the strongest part next to the hinges, like her father always told her to do, and joined her dogs. She took them for a walk, starting at the homeground, through the double ground, the waterground, limekiln, up the sidling into the parrock at the side of the house. She entered the house through the field door.

As well as all the animals, the fields were named and also the farm machinery. Why, Calico did not know. Maybe, as farming could be a lonely life, it helped to familiarise objects with names to give everything a character of its own. The stationary engine was known as Puffing Billy, one of the tractors was named Whistling Rufus, the garden digger Tin Lizzie and so on.

Calico prepared the evening meal ready for her mother and father, when they came in from milking. Her mother was pleased when Calico told her she was seeing William tomorrow.

'Such a nice lad,' her mother said, as Calico knew she would because he was wearing a suit and had reasonably short hair. Her mother did not approve of boys with long hair, pierced ears, leather jackets, and such like. So she was most upset when William arrived the following evening on a motorcycle, and dressed in denim jeans, a leather jacket and a sleeveless denim jacket. Calico was a little amazed herself at the transformation. By way of explanation, William told her that he was driving his father's car yesterday. He wore a suit because his sister had requested it. Calico laughed, she was relieved. She thought he had changed from the William she met at the pop festival, but he was the same person.

Calico enjoyed the evening. William's family were friendly towards her, and she found William good company. He did not kiss her when they said goodnight, because he was shy and did not know what her reaction would be. Calico was disappointed. A typical woman, she was affronted that he did not want to kiss her, and pleased that he had enough respect not to try to kiss her on their first date. William asked if he could take her out again. Calico agreed. He was so different from Charles. She wished she felt the same response to William as she did to Charles. How the chemical reaction between two people was sparked off, she could not imagine. If it was known there would be a lot more sensibly matched couples and a lot less heartache, but the world would not be quite such an intoxicating place to inhabit.

Sunday passed quickly. The family were not regular churchgoers and Sunday on the farm differed little from the rest of the days of the week. The dairy cows still had to be milked; the animals and poultry fed; the eggs collected; the cowstall mucked out. The milk lorry collected the milk the same as every other day. Her father maintained that church was for those who were able to finish their work in six days, and could rest on the seventh. He didn't need to attend church as proof that he believed in God, he was surrounded by His wonders every day on the farm and in the countryside. He watched the animals give birth and the young grow strong. He observed the changing seasons, each in their different apparel: the vivid greens of spring; the greeny-yellow of summer; the red-gold of autumn; the grey-brown of winter. He heard the singing of the birds, and the industrious noise of insects going about their business. He felt the fierce heat of the summer sun on his back, and the bitter biting cold winter wind through his clothes. He smelt the blossom-laden trees, and the air after a long-awaited shower of rain. He tasted milk straight from the udder, and eggs still warm from the nest. He thanked God every day for his good fortune in being able to be free to work alongside nature, and to enjoy his environment.

William had wanted to see Calico again, but today he was apple-picking for his father, who made gallons of rough cider. Calico was returning to Brydle that evening, so he had offered to give her a lift back. He borrowed his father's car, as the warm sunny day had progressed into a wet foggy night. It was cosy in the car, watching the windscreen wipers in their endless task, hearing the drumming of the rain on the roof and the swishing of the wheels. Calico glanced at William's profile when the headlights of other cars lit it up. He was not bad-looking, she thought, not handsome like Charles, but all his features were in proportion, and he had a lovely smile.

Calico directed William to the Mansion House. He stopped the car by the side entrance. They both got out. 'You go on. I'll get your case from the boot and bring it to the door,' William stated.

Calico unlocked the outer door, entered and stood by the inner door. William brought her case in and put it down beside her. Calico thanked him. They stood close together, silent, regarding each other. Calico noticed his shirt clinging to his chest. She reached out and touched it. 'It's damp,' she said. William felt the warmth of her hand through the thin material. It was more than he could stand. He made a move towards her. She came closer. Their lips met. He held her loosely to him, his arms not moving, his hands not roving. Just as suddenly he stopped.

'I'd better go now,' he said quickly. 'I'll give you a ring. Bye.'

'All right,' Calico replied, wondering why the hurry, 'Thanks for the lift.'

He was so gentle, thought Calico. His kisses undemanding, as though his lips were caressing yours. There was no pressure from him. He made you feel warm and relaxed and respected. So different from Charles, who made you feel alive and vital and wanted.

Calico opened the inner door. She did not lock it behind her, as she did not know if Amy was in yet. The parlourmaids had keys to the outer door, but not the inner door. The last one home was to lock the inner door, or if they were all in, then the last one to bed did it. Sophia seldom went out and Calico and Amy left notes, so they would not lock each other out. There was no note on the kitchen table, so Calico left the door unlocked. Scribbled a note to say she was in and went up to her room.

The Lord Mayor was not returning until mid-morning the next day, from her trip to France. The live-in staff were not required to start work until nine o'clock. Amy and Calico had their breakfast together at eight o'clock, to give them plenty of time to catch up with each other's news. Amy had invited John to spend the weekend at her mother's. It did not go too well, her mother did not approve of John, though she was pleasant to him for Amy's sake. He was not the sort she wanted her daughter to associate with. She had failed to fulfil her own ambitious dreams, and now pinned her hopes on her daughter making a successful marriage. She had wanted her to become an actress also, showing no talent or inclination in that direction. She had to settle for her taking a post as a parlourmaid, thinking that she would still be able to meet the right class of person through this kind of work. She did not realise that a parlourmaid's job had lost none of its servant status. A better bet would have been for her to persuade Amy to become a model. They seemed to often marry into the wealthy and titled set. The fact that Amy was happy in her present relationship was not taken into account by her mother. On the concept of happiness Amy and her mother would never agree, that is why their pursuit of it took them in different directions and further from each other. Calico told Amy about meeting William again.

After breakfast the rest of the staff arrived. It did not seem long before it was morning break. There was a lot of chatter today. Grace had plastered her face-powder on thicker than usual, to hide the tell-tale signs of how her weekend had been spent. Susan was on a high because her husband had been with her the whole weekend. Vera's mother had been rushed into hospital and Vera, though worried about her, had been able to do what she wanted over the weekend for a change. The cook had gone to visit her sister and met a nice widower while she was there.

In the middle of these exchanges of information, the head butler's son arrived for the laundry. He had three baskets to collect, which seemed rather a lot as last week had been quiet, someone mentioned. Cook explained that Mr Rolph had told her they had been delivered someone else's laundry by mistake, and he was taking it back today. He had a quick cup of coffee, several slices of toast, and went on his way. The conversation became stilted while he was there. No one cared for him. His attitude was friendly enough, but he tried to use the fact that he was directly related to their boss, expecting his cup of coffee and toast to be ready and waiting for him and leaving his cup and plate for someone else to clear away. He also butted into their conversations and made tactless remarks. They were relieved when he did not stay long. They resumed their chatting until the sound of the front door bell broke them up. This signalled the return of the Lord Mayor. 'Wait for me Charles. I'm going to have a bath, and then you can take me to the hairdresser,' instructed the Lord Mayor. 'Bring the luggage in while you're waiting, save Mr Rolph.'

'Very good Madam,' Charles replied with a cheeky grin. He went to the boot of the car to get out the suitcases, hatboxes, parcels and packages. Something glinting by the laurel hedge caught his eye. He went to investigate. It was a pair of silver sugar tongs. They had the Brydle crest on them, so they must belong to the Mansion House. He slipped them in his pocket. While the Lord Mayor's bath was being prepared, she was going through the appointments diary with her secretary. When Charles had taken all the luggage upstairs, he showed the Mayor the silver tongs he had found. The secretary suggested that maybe the staff could shed some light on it. Charles left them to discuss it and went downstairs to get a cup of coffee. He mentioned his find to cook.

The Lord Mayor was getting into the car, when Mr Rolph came rushing up to inform her that his spare set of keys had gone missing. He said he had only just noticed. The Lord Mayor's secretary decided that in view of the circumstances, he would take an inventory of all the silverware today, now in fact.

By lunchtime the Mansion House was buzzing with the news. Several valuable pieces of silverware were missing, and as soon as the secretary had finished his inventory, he was calling in the police.

Chapter Nine

Amy's Ordeal

> Nature produced us with mutual love, and made us social. According to her laws it is a more wretched thing to do an injury than to suffer death.
>
> Seneca

Calico sat on the wooden seat at the top of the road waiting patiently for Charles to appear. *What a lot of life is spent in waiting*, she thought. *Waiting in queues in shops, banks, post offices. Waiting for people; for transport; for letters; for the end of the working day; for the end of the working week; for the holidays; all sorts of things. Always waiting. No sooner has your waiting been rewarded, than something else arises to be waited for in its place.*

Charles halted the car in front of her and she got into the back. He dropped her off at the same place as previously. He parked the car in its space in front of the Council House and rejoined her. They walked along the street, until Charles stopped outside a wine bar with a garish awning. He opened the door for Calico to enter. Inside it was painted stark white with imitation grape vines and plastic bunches of grapes adorning the walls. Every expense had been spared on the furnishings. There was no covering on the stone floor. The furniture was the plastic garden variety, with bright gingham tablecloths and cushions. The mood was intended to convey a courtyard in France. Calico imagined the scene would be pleasant. Sipping a glass of wine in bright sunlight, the aroma of fresh-baked yeast goods, ground coffee, the scent of flowers, all mingling in the drowsy heat, the birds twittering, the insects busy. But lit by weak electric light bulbs, with the smell of the adjoining Chinese take-away filtering in, on a chilly autumn evening, something had been lost in the transposition.

'Is this more suitable?' Charles asked.

Calico nodded assent. Charles fetched them a bottle of wine and two glasses. They sat down.

'Were you questioned by the police?' Calico whispered. Not having much to do with the police, only the local copper when he called to inspect the movement book on the farm, she was over-awed by the situation.

'Yes. It was me that found the sugar tongs and started the ball rolling,' answered Charles, pleased with himself as if he had done an heroic deed.

'How exciting!' exclaimed Calico. 'It was just like you see on the television. The place swarming with police and being questioned about your whereabouts the night before.'

'Well, they would make a fuss. The silver belongs to the people of the city,' retorted Charles. 'The City Council will want to get it back before too many people hear about it. They are responsible for it.

'It's embarrassing really. They need to interview everyone who was near the Mansion House last night,' confessed Calico with a grimace.

'Why's that embarrassing?' questioned Charles.

'Because I had to give the name and address of the person who gave me a lift back last night. I don't know what he'll think when the police turn up on his doorstep,' explained Calico.

'He! Who brought you back?' demanded Charles frowning. 'William,' answered Calico, adding quickly, 'A friend.'

'A boyfriend?' asked Charles vehemently.

'I don't know. Not exactly,' floundered Calico, startled by his intense outburst. Charles then proceeded to question her about William. How long had she known him? Where had they met? How old was he? How often did they meet and so on? It seemed to upset him.

'I don't question you about your wife,' Calico snapped at last, exasperated with his attitude. It could not have been more effective if she had slapped his face. He went silent. The telephone jangled out harshly. It was for Charles, the Lord Mayor's meeting had finished, he was needed.

'I'll come back here and pick you up. I won't be long, wait for me,' he said quietly.

Calico waited, she wondered what his mood would be when he returned. She did not have long to wait. He must have got the Lord Mayor home in record time. 'Come on,' he urged her as soon as he neared the table. 'Let's go.' Calico obeyed. They drove for a while in silence.

'Where are we going?' queried Calico finally.

'To put the car away,' said Charles curtly.

'Back to the Mansion House?'

'No. The car is garaged at the City Council depot, on the outskirts of the City.'

Charles drew up in front of a pair of large wrought iron gates. He gave four toots on the horn. A light went on, a man came out of a little wooden hut the other side of the gates, and opened them up. As Charles drove through, Calico saw the man smile and wink at him. The man shut the gates, went back inside the hut and turned off the light.

Charles expertly manoeuvred the Daimler backwards into the garage. He turned off the engine and switched on the interior light. He looked at Calico. He pulled her roughly to him and kissed her.

'I've been wanting to do that all evening,' he said huskily. 'Let's go in the back.'

'No,' said Calico firmly. 'I'd rather stay here.' Charles was disappointed, she was giving him a hard time. She was obviously going to be no pushover.

Still, she's here, that's a start, he thought, kissing her again. After a while Calico decided it was time to make a move. It was getting late. Charles reluctantly agreed, realising he could not get any further with her tonight. They got out of the car. Charles put on the garage light, walked over to a red van and unlocked the doors. He held open the passenger door for Calico, she got in. He put out the garage light, got into the van and drove to the wrought iron gates where he performed the same ritual as before.

We do not have conversations, thought Calico on the way back. With Charles it was more actions than words. She found herself wondering what he would be like to live with, would they talk then, or would Charles still see no need for words? He stopped the van at the top of the Mansion House road. He kissed her goodnight. 'I'm sorry I behaved badly tonight,' he murmured. 'I was jealous at the thought of you with someone else. You don't realise how I feel about you. Can I see you Friday?'

As usual, against her better judgement, Calico said yes. When he was kissing and caressing her, and sending all sorts of delightful feelings through her body, she wanted to see him again. As soon as she was apart from him doubts crept in. Neither wanted to be the one to end their time together. Time after time they said goodnight to each other, but did not part. The church clock chimed one.

'Oh no!' exclaimed Calico. 'I'm supposed to be in by midnight.'

'Why, do you turn into a pumpkin? Never mind, you've got a key,' shrugged Charles.

'I've got to go, Charles, goodnight.'

'Night love. I'll be counting the hours.'

Calico hurried down the road to the Mansion House. She unlocked the outer door of the staff entrance safe inside, she locked it behind her. She gently turned the knob on the inner door, so as not to make a noise, and pushed. It did not move. Help, thought Calico, it's locked. What could she do? She could not ring the bell, no one would hear it downstairs. She could not go to the front door and ring that bell, or she would be in trouble with the Lord Mayor. *I know*, she thought, *I'll telephone Amy to let me in.* The telephone was put through to the staff quarters after ten o'clock at night so it would not disturb the Mayor if it rang in the night. The telephone was situated in a cubby hole by Amy's door, she would be bound to hear it. The nearest telephone box was a couple of streets away.

Calico drew back the bolts she had just put in place on the outer door and stepped out into the night. She had not noticed how cold it was, previously she had been in a hurry and the warmth of the van had stayed with her. The street lights were out. There was minimal light from a veiled moon, similar to the one in Coleridge's poem *Christabel*, thought Calico. She shivered as she recalled the words of the poem. She had to steel herself to walk past the churchyard. Determined not to look towards the gravestones, but expecting at any moment to see or hear something frightful. At home in the country Calico was unafraid of the dark. She often walked down the lonely dark country lanes on her own, coming home from a village dance, or the last bus. It never worried her. There were always sounds, but she could recognise them, a cow coughing; the hoot of an owl; the bark of a dog fox and the answering call of the vixen. All the noises could be explained away. The rustling in the hedge would be a cat playing with its prey, a hedgehog rooting for food, or she sometimes caught a glimpse of a badger's backside disappearing into the hedge if the moon was bright. She did not feel alone with all that activity going on around her. Here in the city, all was silent, unnerving. It was creepy, there was nowhere to hide.

Once, on her way home from a dance in the village, she was approached by a man in a car who offered her a lift home. She declined and told him she did not live far away. He asked where. She pointed to a rank of houses and lied, 'The end one there.' This seemed to satisfy him and he drove off. She turned off the main road into the country lanes that led to her home. She took the right hand lane at the fork. She had not gone far, when she heard a car behind her. She looked back and saw the car's headlights going up the hill of the left-hand lane. It turned around at the top and started back down the hill. Calico ran for the nearest gate, jumped over it, and hid behind the hedge, in the field. The car came slowly by her. Calico stayed low. She heard the car turning, it came back past her and it must have gone out on to the main road. Calico did not know this city area; there were no field hedges to protect her here.

Thankfully she reached the telephone box. It rang for ages before Amy answered. She sounded drowsy. Calico explained what had happened. Amy said she would go down and unlock the door straight away.

Calico hurried back to the Mansion House. Her head down, looking neither right nor left, but her ears straining for any sound that would warn her of impending danger. She was wearing a dark mauve midi coat with a hood, that hid most of her face. She resembled in outline the dark figure of a monk. She would have been more likely to frighten people in her pathway, than they her. Gliding silently along like a spectre, she reached the outer door.

The inner door was still locked when she tried it. Amy must have gone straight back to bed after she answered the telephone. Calico did not relish the idea of making another nocturnal journey to the telephone box, and there was still no guarantee Amy would unlock the door. She could not break the glass of the door to reach the lock, that would be too desperate.

There was only one thing to do. She would have to sleep here, between the two doors, tonight. She took the coconut matting from the doorstep and laid it on the stone floor, to lie on. She took off her coat and her outer jumper. She rolled up her jumper, put it on the step for a pillow, led on the matting, and pulled her coat over her for a blanket. She slept fitfully. It was cold and uncomfortable but at least it was safe and sheltered. Every time she awoke she wondered where she was with such an unyielding pillow, a scratchy mattress, and a thin covering. *Even in this state I must be better off than some people*, she thought.

Luckily Amy was the first downstairs the next morning. She feigned surprise when she found Calico lying in between the doorways.

'Don't look so amazed Amy. I rang you last night to open the door for me. Remember?' Calico said annoyed.

'I'm sorry. I'm hopeless at waking up. I was half-asleep on the telephone. I must have gone back to bed and forgotten,' explained Amy apologetically.

'Thanks a lot, Amy,' said Calico, rushing past her. 'I'd better hurry if I'm to be down in the kitchen on time.'

The following evening Calico found out who was responsible for locking her out. Amy was out, Calico was on duty, and Sophia, as usual, was glued to the television. Calico watched the television for an hour after she finished work, and then told Sophia she was going to bed.

''Ave you lock door?' questioned Sophia abruptly.

'No. Amy out,' answered Calico.

'I do when I go bed,' stated Sophia. 'Mr Rolph say midnight secure now.'

Calico went upstairs to her bedroom. She undressed and got into bed; but she could not sleep. She was half listening for Amy. She put on the bedside light and read while she waited. She heard footfalls on the stairs; they sounded heavy and solid like Sophia's. She heard the stair door open and close. The footsteps passed by Amy's door. That must be Sophia. *Bitch*, Calico thought, *it would give Sophia the greatest delight to lock Amy out, and get her into trouble just as she tried to do to me last night. If she was not so lazy at getting up in the mornings, her nasty action would have worked.*

Calico waited half an hour to give Sophia time to finish her ablutions and to get into bed. Then she rose and put a coat over her night attire. Softly, with slippered feet, she stole downstairs to unlock the inner door for Amy. Calico was not prepared for the scene that awaited her. Amy was sat huddled by the door, sobbing loudly. Calico was amazed that she was so upset about being locked out.

'It's all right,' she soothed. 'I've come down to let you in.' Amy apparently had not heard Calico unlock the door. She looked up at her vacantly.

'It's all right,' Calico repeated. 'Don't cry so. You can come in now, the door's unlocked.'

'It's not all right,' spat out Amy vehemently. 'It'll never be all right ever again.' And she returned to her sobbing. Suddenly she stood up, as if only just realising the door was open. There was a wild look on her face. 'The bathroom. I must get to the bathroom. I'll wash it all away in the bath, soak it out of my system,' she rambled, as she rushed past Calico. 'That's what I'll do.'

Calico was stupefied. Whatever was the matter with Amy? Her face had been terrifying to look upon. Her eyes had an insane glint in them. Her mouth contorted into a maniacal grin. Her hair was in violent disarray. What tragedy could have befallen her to change her features so dramatically? Calico in her worst nightmares would not be able to conjure up in her imagination the ordeal Amy had been through that evening.

Amy had met John that afternoon. John usually borrowed a car from someone to take Amy out, but he had been unable to do so that day. The sky had opened and the rain had poured down. They both got soaked walking from the bus stop to the shopping centre. John suggested they went back to his flat. Amy had never been there before. He did not like to take her there, but he could not think what else to do. It was not a nice area where he lived. It was an estate of high-rise flats – all the city's miscreants were congregated there.

Inside the flat, Amy and John took off their wet clothes. Amy got into the bed to keep warm, while John took their clothes downstairs, to dry them in the basement laundry. He came back with a key. Amy was mystified.

'I've put them in the tumble dryer, they'll take a while. The key is for the padlock on the tumble dryer, I have to lock it up or our clothes would disappear,' John explained as he joined her in the bed. They cuddled together to get warmth from each other's body heat. They kissed, gently at first, and then ardently. Amy was pleased that the love-making was happening so naturally, giving her time to feel aroused. She had not felt like this with anyone before. She really wanted him, wanted to feel him inside her. She mounted him and sat back on her heels astride him, looking down at his face. John's eyes were closed, his mouth was half open; suddenly the door burst open, someone came up behind Amy. She felt the coldness, the sharpness, of a metal blade resting against her ribs. She heard a voice snarl, 'Just do as I tell you and I won't have to use the knife.'

Amy froze. John was still inside her, the other man knelt behind her and pushed his hardness up into her as well. Amy gasped and shouted at John to do something. He replied, 'Don't worry it won't hurt you if you don't struggle.' All hope went from Amy, John was agreeing to it.

'Come on you bitch,' growled the man from behind. 'Bounce up and down, I want to feel something, move it.' He grabbed her breast with his free hand and squeezed hard. Amy screamed out, which made him thrust more fiercely into her. He took a piece of cloth out of his shirt pocket, and, still with the knife in his hand, gagged her with it. 'That'll keep you quiet, we don't want anyone to hear your screams and come in and join our fun, do we?' he said menacingly. 'Now when I squeeze your nipple hard that means down, when I let go that means up. Okay, let's try it.'

Amy sobbed, they took no notice; intent on their pleasure. She could feel the knife blade pressed against her and gave in. Up and down, up and down, 'Faster bitch faster,' barked the man with the knife. Both men were panting heavily. 'Come on ride us bitch, take us all the way, finish us off, harder, you're not taking us in deep enough, you gotta take every inch in.' He dropped the knife as he used both hands to manoeuvre himself into the best position for maximum effect. He was losing control of his senses engulfed in pleasure. Amy seized her chance. Abruptly she stopped moving, climbed off of them, and reached for the knife. The man grabbed her hands and held them behind her back. 'No you don't, we haven't finished,' he snapped. He took a length of cord from his pocket and tied her hands behind her back. He picked up the knife. He removed her gag. 'Please no, no more, not again, let me go,' begged Amy. 'You stopped before we were satisfied. That was very naughty of you,' he scolded in a quietly threatening tone. 'So now I'll have to keep an eye on you while we do it. Kneel on the floor by the end of the bed. Now.' He sat on the bed in front of her.

'I'll scream,' Amy threatened. 'Let me go or I will.'

'You won't,' he answered, smiling. 'You'll have your mouth full, get your lips around that.' He stuck his male organ into her face, and the knife towards her throat. As he was doing this, John approached her from behind, she felt him enter her, and start thrusting away. The other man put the knife down beside him, took Amy's head between his hands and held on to it, while he pushed himself in and out of her mouth. Amy thought she might choke, it was huge. When he got the rhythm going, he moved one of his hands to her breasts, holding a nipple between finger and thumb he squeezed as hard as he could, twisting it at the same time. Amy screamed, but no sound came out. The man laughed nastily, 'Aah, mmm, that's nice, your scream tickles the end of my prick. Come on harden up those nipples make like you're enjoying it.' And every time he pushed into her mouth, he squeezed hard on her nipple, first one breast then the other. He was relentless. She was gasping for breath. He pulled out of her. She groaned. Before she could say anything he knelt in front of her, took her head firmly in his hands and kissed her; pushing his tongue far into her mouth, nearly suffocating her and stifling her screams, as he forced his way into her beside John, who with a long moan and several swear words, signified it was over for him.

'Don't worry John, you can have her again in a while.'

'Don't you think she's had enough?' ventured John.

'She might have, but I haven't,' the other man replied, as he climaxed and pulled out of Amy. He replaced the gag, dragged her on to the bed, and untied her hands. Amy was relieved, thinking her ordeal over. But no. He then tied her hands and feet to the bed posts. Left her there, naked and spreadeagled, while they sat beside her and smoked a cigarette.

Amy felt degraded and humiliated. They were discussing her as if she was just a body there for their pleasure. Something without a face or feelings. So wrapped up were they in their own pleasure and lustful feelings. Women did not mean very much to them as people in their own right. Only as a body to be used, abused, and cast aside for the next one. Amy wondered how many times they had done this before.

'I reckon I'll stick it up her one more time,' the other man was saying. 'I haven't had much luck with women lately. Might as well make the most of this piece while she's laid out ready, and got no choice.'

'We haven't set nothing up like this for a while,' said John. 'The last one we did together was that prostitute I brought home.'

The other man laughed harshly, 'The most work she'd ever done in a night. We had her humping us without a break, like a rabbit, then Blackhead, Forklift and Hoss took her next door to a party.'

'Boy was she wasted by the time we'd finished with her,' said John smiling.

'Serves her right,' sneered the other man. 'Expecting us to pay for what nature's given her. Exploiting it like it was something special and worth money. You're lucky girlie, we're treating you well, and doing most of the work, 'cos you don't trade on it against men.'

If Amy's mouth had not been gagged it would have fallen open at that last remark. The word lucky was not in Amy's vocabulary at the moment. It was certainly not how she would describe herself in this situation. It made it even more difficult for her to understand the mentality of the other man, who thought he was treating her well.

The men started to move. Amy shut her eyes, steeling herself against what would happen next.

'You going first?' asked John.

'Yes,' the other man replied, climbing on top of Amy and ruthlessly ramming into her with brutal force. John kissed and gnawed at her nipples and neck. He whispered in her ear, 'I'm sorry love, I've got no choice. I've got to go along with Silver or he'd turn nasty.' He could taste the salty tears running silently down her cheeks.

The other man, who John had referred to as Silver, seemed to be going on forever, with long deep thrusting strokes he battered his way into Amy. She passed out. John slapped her face to try and bring her round.

'Keep her conscious John. I might as well do it with a blow up dolly, if she's going to be out of it,' Silver complained.

'Come on baby, you can't let us down now, keep awake. The more you pass out, the longer it's going to take him, and I'm ready for my turn; so if you don't concentrate real hard I'm going to get desperate, and shove it in your mouth and make you choke on it,' warned John, trying to convince Amy that it would be in her interests to stay conscious. *Surely they are not human*, she thought. Eventually Silver finished, and John took over.

John decided he wanted to try it lots of different ways. He tossed her and turned her, stood her on her head, bent her over backwards, with the assistance of Silver, who, while supporting her, suggested other positions. Amy tried to become disengaged from her body, to stand back and look at it as if it was happening to somebody else. It was the only way she could cope with it. *It can't go on forever*, she kept thinking. She was aching all over. It felt as though they had flung her down, and trampled all over her body. She kept passing in and out of consciousness. Every time she came round she was sure it had been a nightmare; but they were still there: she could still feel them, still hear them. *I'm going to die*, she thought with relief, *they're going to ride me to death. I won't have to think about this day, I won't have to live with it for the rest of my life, for I won't be here*. Death seemed so sweet to Amy then, like a blessed release. She would be at peace. No one pulling at her, pushing into her, pawing her. *God, if you love me you'll take me now*, she said to herself, as she slipped into unconsciousness again.

Amy woke up alone in the half-light. She wrapped herself in the bedsheet. She felt ill. She struggled to the bathroom and was violently sick. She desperately wanted a bath, but she dare not in case they came back. She had to get away. She could hear the people in the next flat through the partition. There was a lot of laughing and cheering, and a scream that was cut short. 'Shut up bitch. I told you she couldn't take you all on.' Amy recognised the voice of the other man that raped her, even though it was slurred, there was still that underlying tone of contempt in it for the female sex. She heard him say, 'I know a tasty little piece that we enjoyed earlier tonight. She's locked in John's flat, we let her sleep it off, she'll be ready again by now. I'll just take my turn with this one and then I'll go and fetch her.'

Amy tensed as she heard a key turn in the lock. She looked around for a weapon to defend herself. 'Amy,' whispered John's voice. 'Amy quick.'

She came out of the bathroom. 'Don't say anything. Here's your clothes. Dress quickly, get out this window, and down the fire escape, and be quiet. I think you've taken enough for one night. I'll lock the door again on my way out. I'll meet you at the bottom of the steps. Wait for me, don't run for it, this is a bad area. I'll take you home.'

Amy did not know what to do. She had to get out of the room, that was for sure, but go with John? He had been like an animal, (no, animals don't behave that badly), like a lust-crazed being who had lost his reason, steeped only in his own greedy pleasure, using her any which way he could to reap the utmost ecstasy. It seemed to move him to greater heights of fulfilment to share her with someone else, made it easier for him to forget she was a person in her own right, and not a sexual vehicle for his passion to be vented on until it was sated.

John must have moved quickly; he was probably scared what the others would do to him, if they sussed out what he was up to; for he was waiting at the bottom of the fire escape. He grabbed Amy's arm before she could say anything. 'Come on,' he said urgently. 'Run like hell, run like your life depended on it, 'cos it might.' She ran with all the strength she could muster. John guided her towards a garage.

'Wait here,' he ordered her. He knocked at the door of a nearby house, a mean-looking man answered the knock, they exchanged words and the man handed something to John and shut the door. John joined Amy. 'Okay,' he said unlocking the garage door. 'We've got transport.' He unlocked the car, got in and opened the passenger's door for Amy. 'Get in,' he urged, 'And stay low. They're probably looking for you. They'll think you won't have got far on foot and they can catch you up, and drag you back to their all night drinking session.'

'Won't you get into trouble?' Amy asked hopefully.

'No. When they can't find you, they'll pick up some other unsuspecting female, probably a pro from a street corner, to use instead. As long as they find someone, they'll have forgotten about it by morning. One is as good as another to them; they don't remember the names or the faces; that's not what they're interested in,' he replied. 'You can sit up now, we're out on the main road.'

'How could you do it to me? I thought you liked me,' Amy asked him, now the enormity of what she had been through hit her, and the realisation of the escape she had just had. She sobbed. Great heaving sobs racked her body, she could not stop them.

'I do like you,' he answered. 'I wouldn't be risking my neck for you if I didn't. I would have left you to the mercy of the others. I suppose what we did was out of order, I got carried away, caught up in the moment. Then I had to make sure you were exhausted and passed out, or Silver would have taken you with us to the people in the next flat.'

Here I am in this dishevelled sorry state, thought Amy, *and he as good as tells me he's done me a favour.*

John stopped the car in the road outside the Mansion House entrance gates. Amy made no attempt to get out of the car. She could not leave it like this. She had to tell him how she felt to try to make him understand what an evil act he had committed.

'If it wasn't for you none of this would have happened. How can you calmly sit there after what you did to me, you put me through hell, and you don't even realise it. I would gladly have died tonight; I felt so repulsed, so sickened, so ashamed, as if in some way I was partly responsible for the atrocities you were committing on my body. I wanted to escape anyway I could; dying meant escape, and I wanted to die,' Amy cried, uncontrollably and hysterically, as if her flood of tears would wash the incident out of her mind. There was no reply from John. His knuckles were white as he clenched the steering wheel. She had not been able to bring herself to look at him before, but he was so quiet, she took a sidelong glance at him. His face was as white as his knuckles, and he was biting his lip. He said quietly, 'We must have been rough on you. I didn't mean to hurt you, I'm really sorry, I thought you could take it.'

'You still don't understand, do you?' she screamed at him. 'Everything's physical with you: you did hurt me, yes, but the physical scars will heal, it's the mental pain I can't bear, that will be with me forever. What happened tonight is over for you, it was over as soon as the physical sensations subsided. It'll never be over for me. It'll be with me for my lifetime, in my head, recurring in my nightmares. I'll never be free of it. You've ruined me and ruined the rest of my life. If I could be granted a wish, apart from wishing it had never happened, I wish you could be made to feel as I do now, that you would have to shoulder this burden for the rest of your life, that it would haunt you, as it will haunt me, to the grave.'

'Don't say any more,' he interrupted her. 'I can't stand it. I've never taken a girl home afterwards. I never realised, they always looked okay when I seen them in the street a few days later.'

'On the outside, inside they're crying. To you it's a sexual act, to us it's an emotional trauma. We can't deal with it, we've been conditioned by society that sex is part of a loving relationship, performed with mutual consent. Then along you come and hit our emotions all to hell, by forcing sex upon us, treating us like worthless nonentities. We can't cope. We feel like social outcasts, defiled, stained, violated, blemished, not able to return to our normal lives. Through no fault of our own, we've broken society's moral rules of conduct, and we have to suffer. We either tell no one and it festers away in the back of our minds, or we tell the police and have to relive the moments again and again as we're questioned. Our personal lives are probed into, and the whole world knows our shame. Either way we're losers. There is no punishment that can be done to you, that could undo the harm you've done. No torment that could equal the killing of another person's emotions, no amount of suffering could repay for loss of a normal happy life. You'll never begin to understand what you've done. For a night of lust, you've subjected me to a life of misery. Nothing will ever be the same again,' wailed Amy.

'Being a bit dramatic, aren't we?' cajoled John.

'You've changed my whole outlook on life. I used to trust the world, and whatever it meted out to me, I was sure it wouldn't be that bad, and I could overcome it. But not this, this is a shock I can't recover from. Never can I let my guard down again, never can I trust again. What am I going to do? How am I going to get through life?' and she broke down crying again. 'I could kill you for what you've done to me, but what good would that do? It wouldn't change things, it's too late. I just hope that your life is as miserable as it can possibly be, and nothing ever goes right for you.'

'It won't change much then. My life's miserable now,' he replied. 'I'm unemployed, all me mates are drugged up or drunk most of the time, to try and shut out their problems. I suppose it doesn't excuse what we do, but the only time you can really lose yourself is when you're screwing: nothing else matters as you lose your senses and become totally immersed in obtaining as much pleasure as you can, and maintaining it for as long as possible. It takes over mind and body. The female becomes just a blurr, as you use her body in whatever way gives you the utmost satisfaction. It's the only way we can get pleasure that costs nothing.'

'It costs our sanity,' retorted Amy acidly.

'I never thought about it from the woman's point of view. Seeing how upset you are, what you've said. I'm going to get away from here, start a new life away from me mates. I can't change them, but I can change. There must be a job for me somewhere. I didn't realise what I was doing, the women I've harmed. It became common practice that whoever had a woman for a night, the others that didn't have one, shared.'

'How awful,' Amy said aghast. 'You mean no woman could enter your block of flats safely?'

'Sometimes, if everybody's coupled. You were unlucky tonight, Silver's woman let him down and he must have heard us,' answered John.

'Why's he called Silver?' Amy asked.

'I would have thought that was obvious,' grinned John. 'The size of his... you must have noticed.'

'It still hasn't got through to you; you're still making light of it,' said Amy, despairingly. 'I've got to get out of this car. I can't think straight. I don't know what I'm going to do.'

'Sorry love,' said John, feebly. 'I don't suppose you'll want to see me again.'

Amy looked at him amazed. Her face contorted with rage, 'After what you did. I hate you,' she spat at him as she got out of the car and slammed the door. John drove off.

Calico knocked softly on the bathroom door.

'Amy can I come in?' she asked, concerned for her friend. Amy did not answer. Calico could hear her crying. 'Amy unlock the door.' Calico was worried after seeing the look on Amy's face as she had rushed past her. 'Amy please.' Calico heard the key turn in the lock. She opened the door.

Amy's face was calmer, but there was still a disturbed gleam in her eyes. 'Oh Calico!' she exclaimed. 'What am I going to do? Remember what your mother told you, about nothing in this world that can't be faced. Well, she's wrong. I can't face up to this.'

'Whatever's the matter Amy?' said Calico mystified.

Amy ignored her question, if indeed she heard it at all. 'All the details are printed in my mind, stamped there forever. I'll never get over it. I feel so awful. I can still imagine them all over me.' She shuddered. 'It's horrible, horrible, horrible. I tried to wash them away, but they're still there, still imprinted.'

Calico could not understand any of Amy's ramblings. 'What Amy, what is it? Amy answer me.' Calico insisted.

'I've been raped, Calico, *raped*, me,' said Amy hysterically sobbing again.

'Oh no!' exclaimed Calico on a sharp intake of breath. 'How, who, phone the police, tell them.'

'I can't,' stated Amy hopelessly. 'I can't go through all the questioning, relive it all again in words. They probably won't believe me anyway. I was in John's flat, in bed, naked, when it happened. They won't treat it seriously. They'll say I was asking for trouble, being in that area in the first place. I didn't know what it was like. There's nothing I can do. Absolutely nothing. I've no proof, there are no marks on me. They'll ask why I didn't struggle. I was so scared I did what I was told.'

Calico realised Amy was right, her story would not sound convincing. In bed, naked, no evidence of force being used. Yet she knew Amy, and she knew Amy would not be in the state she was if it had happened with her consent. But the police look at the facts, and they were not in Amy's favour. It did not seem right that the people who had destroyed Amy's sanity, could not be made accountable for their actions and would go free, when Amy never would be. And Calico feeling frustrated by her inability to help and the injustice of the situation, cried alongside Amy.

From that day Amy changed. She ceased to live inwardly. Her mind went blank. She put herself into an automated state. Her character was passive and remote, switched off from thinking and feeling. She did everything as though in a dream. She did not want to wake up to the reality of her situation. To get through another day was an ordeal. She turned against her body, as though in some way it was responsible. She never bothered to make up her face, she wore baggy clothes to hide her figure, she cut her hair short and spent all her off-duty time in her room.

It upset Calico greatly. She remembered the Amy of the pop festival and the starched underwear prank. The careless, laughing, extrovert Amy. Tears pricked the back of Calico's eyes whenever she looked at the pathetic creature Amy had become. Calico wished the people who committed rape could see what a lasting effect it had on the victim. It was easy for them to be casual and think nothing more about it, when the person was detached from them. She wished you could somehow put a dream in their head when they were sleeping where they saw a woman they loved, like a mother, sister, wife, or daughter, gradually deteriorate mentally after being subjected to sex against their will. To see the emotional decay taking effect, long after the physical signs have disappeared.

Chapter Ten

A Skeleton in the Cupboard

> It many times falls out that we deem ourselves much deceived in others, because we first deceived ourselves.
>
> Sir P. Sidney

The police had questioned all the household staff on the day the Mansion House silver was reported missing. They were now questioning previous staff, and anybody with a remote connection to the Mansion House. The kitchen hummed with gossip and chatter. Speculations on who could have taken it, when it was taken, and so on, were discussed at length. The cook had met a former parlourmaid in the shopping centre the previous day. She was anxious to re-tell their conversation. When everyone was gathered together at breaktime she began to impart her news. 'I met Jane yesterday afternoon in the centre.'

'Jane?' quizzed Susan.

'She used to be a parlourmaid here, before you came. The others know who I mean,' answered Cook impatiently.

'We know who you mean. Nasty business that,' stated Vera wryly.

'What?' asked Susan.

'She doesn't want to know about that,' began Cook.

'I do,' interrupted Susan. 'Go on, tell me.'

The older staff exchanged glances. Calico wanted to know too, but kept quiet.

'It's over and done with,' said Cook firmly.

'Everyone else knew at the time,' put in Grace. 'So what does it matter.'

'Tell me,' insisted Susan. 'You may as well, you know I won't rest now until I know.'

'I'm not going to be the one to tell, it might not have been true,' said Cook evasively.

'I don't know this Jane, so I'm not likely to repeat it to her,' cajoled Susan.

'All right,' agreed Grace. 'But this is on the understanding that what I tell you was only hearsay.' Susan nodded agreement, not wishing to interrupt the flow now Grace had started. 'There was talk that Jane had an affair with the chauffeur,' confided Grace.

Is that it?' Susan inquired incredulous. 'If the chauffeur was Charles I wouldn't blame her. He is rather fanciable.'

'It was Charles,' answered Grace. 'And that isn't all. She became pregnant and had an abortion, he paid for it.'

There was silence as this piece of information was digested. Calico did not want to believe it. Cook admitted it might not be true, and Grace did say it was only hearsay, she thought. She had an awful dread in the pit of her stomach.

'Jane was telling me that the police had interviewed her. Then they went to see the chap she was going out with, when she worked here,' Cook had seized her chance and had at last managed to monopolise the conversation. 'Apparently, when Jane was living here, her chap had another door key cut, so that he could creep in through the staff entrance and up to her room. The inner door was never locked then, security wasn't as tight. So he came and went as he pleased.'

'That must put him high on the list of suspects,' said Vera. Mr Rolph entered the kitchen. Cook repeated what she had told the others to him.

'I suspected as much,' commented Mr Rolph. 'Never trusted the lad. I did find a few things went missing when Jane worked here.'

'You never mentioned it,' rejoined Cook.

'I was never that certain. I had no proof, just my suspicions,' countered Mr Rolph, self-righteously.

'Looks as though you may have been right.'

Well that was that, thought Calico. Mr Rolph and Cook, being judge and jury, had found him guilty. Take him out and hang him in the morning.

'Do you think he still has the silver on him?' wondered Cook. 'It would be nice to get it back.'

'Probably,' replied Mr Rolph. 'It will not be that easy to dispose of it locally, with our crest emblazoned on it, unless he knows the right people.'

The rest of the staff were disappointed. This was the end of the excitement. No more visits from the police to interrupt their duties. No more speculations. So, without any verification from an official source, they resigned themselves to the fact Jane's former boyfriend had been the thief, and that was an end to it.

One or two of the staff commented on the change in Amy: how quiet and subdued she had become, how difficult it was to talk to her. They decided it was because she was upset about breaking up with her boyfriend. They left her alone; thinking she would get over it and be her old self again. But they could not explain away the odd look in her eyes. It was not discussed, each believing they were the only ones to see it. Amy had told no one else but Calico about being raped. She felt ashamed of what had happened to her. Calico wanted to tell Tryphena, she felt she knew so much on the subject of sordidness in the world, she would be able to help. She could talk to Amy from her own experiences and maybe put her in contact with someone in similar circumstances. Amy made Calico promise not to tell anyone at all about it. Calico could only agree when people said John was to blame for the state Amy was in; they did not know the half of it, but Calico's lips were sealed.

Calico met Charles at the usual place on Friday evening. She found it hard not to start questioning him straight away, concerning what Grace had divulged. She waited until they were seated in a quiet corner of the wine bar, before she began her interrogation.

'Charles,' she said looking fixedly at him.

'Yes my lover,' he replied brightly.

She wished he would not use that expression when addressing her. 'Do you remember Jane?'

'Jane?' queried Charles non-committal, his face giving nothing away.

'Jane, who used to be a parlourmaid,' prompted Calico.

'Oh! That Jane. Yes, vaguely. The police questioned me again today,' he said changing the subject. 'Did they question your friend, um William, wasn't it?'

Calico ignored his question, and pursued with her own. 'Vaguely? That was the word you used, vaguely.'

'Yes. It was a few years ago, and she didn't stay at the Mansion House long,' said Charles irritated by her probing.

'But long enough for you to have an affair with her?' snapped Calico nastily.

'Who told you that?' asked Charles taken aback.

'Did you?' persisted Calico, keeping her eyes on his.

'It wasn't really an affair. We only went out a couple of times, then I called a halt to it,' admitted Charles, trying to make light of it.

'Only a couple of times,' repeated Calico stressing each word.

'It wasn't much more than that,' replied Charles. 'It didn't mean anything.'

'And was she pregnant when the affair finished?' asked Calico in a lowered voice.

Charles frowned, a hopeless look came into his eyes, he shrugged his shoulders. 'I don't know,' he finally answered, shaking his head.

'You don't know,' hissed Calico.

'No. She told me she was pregnant about a month after we stopped seeing each other. She said she didn't know if it was mine or her current boyfriend's, but she was having an abortion anyway. Her boyfriend didn't have any money. She wanted me to pay for it, or she would tell my wife about our affair, and that the baby was mine.'

'And you gave her the money,' interceded Calico.

'And I gave her the money. I had no choice. I don't even know if she really was pregnant,' said Charles dejectedly. How clever he was, in the course of the conversation he had gone from being a complete cad to becoming the injured party. Gaining Calico's sympathy on the way. This man was wasted, he had missed his true vocation in life; he should have been a politician at the very least.

'So she sort of blackmailed you?' ventured Calico.

'Yes, I suppose you could call it that,' agreed Charles. The blacker he painted Jane's character, the better it made him look in contrast.

'Do you make a point of going out with the parlourmaids? Is it a tradition or something?' Calico wanted to know.

'Of course not,' lied Charles. 'I only went out with her because we happened to be at the same party one night. I walked her back to the Mansion House, and one thing led to another, like it does when you've had one drink too many.'

'Oh really!' said Calico, sarcastically. 'And that was all there was to it; a drunken encounter. And I suppose you were also drunk every time you saw each other again.'

'Something like that,' murmured Charles sheepishly.

'What a fool I've been. Will I get the old heave-ho, when you get your way and then tire of me?' enquired Calico, caustically.

'You can't compare what we have with the casual meetings I had with her,' insisted Charles. 'It's completely different.'

'I think it would be better if we didn't see each other any more outside of working hours,' returned Calico in an icy voice.

Charles crossed his fingers behind his back, and steadied his voice for his next speech. 'Don't say that. I love you Calico, you must know I do,' he said, hoping to sound sincere. 'You mean more to me than anything. Please don't turn me away I couldn't bear it. If you deny me you might as well kill me, I'll be dead inside. I want you so much, I think of you all the time. Please don't let this affect us. I regret it ever happened. I need you to live.'

'Give the man an Oscar, a performance like that should not go unrewarded,' sneered Calico coldly, remaining unmoved. 'I'll catch a bus back to the Mansion House. I need time to think, away from you.' She got up from her seat preparing to go.

'Please Calico no, don't go like this. At least let me walk with you to the bus stop,' pleaded Charles, thinking once outside in his arms, she would succumb to his charms again, and he could talk her round. The telephone rang. It was for Charles; he went to answer it. When he came back Calico had gone. *Damn*, he thought. What an awkward business it was going out with virgins. You had to treat them so carefully not to upset their sensibilities. Still, his wife would be pleased. He would be home early now. The feelings Calico aroused in him had to be vented on someone, and his wife never refused his advances. She would be in luck tonight, he was in the mood to make love for hours. He would close his eyes and imagine it was Calico underneath him: her body he was kissing and caressing with his hands, his lips, his tongue. Her moans and gasps of pleasure as he expertly brought her to a climax. He knew he was a good lover, he wished Calico would let him show her how good. He finished his drink and went to collect the Lord Mayor.

Meanwhile Calico was back in her bedroom, sifting through her thoughts, trying to sort out what she felt for Charles, which seemed something akin to madness the way it possessed her when in close proximity to him. She was glad she was going home over the Christmas period. The Lord Mayor and her consort were away for the two weeks. All the staff had been given the time off, and the Mansion House would be closed. Sophia would be staying with Maria and her husband. Calico asked Amy if she would like to spend Christmas with her at the farm. Amy declined, saying she and her mother were spending Christmas together, the first in a long time. Amy was looking forward to it, she would confide in her mother, she was sure she could help her. Tryphena was spending her Christmas in London with relatives.

Calico did not see Charles to speak to properly before she left for the holiday. She was relieved. He was annoyed.

Chapter Eleven

Christmas at Home

Calico had forgotten how cold it was in the old farmhouse. When she awoke her bedroom windows were patterned with ice. There was no heating upstairs. All the bedrooms had firegrates, but the fires were only lit if someone was ill in bed. Downstairs the only warm room was the kitchen, where the Rayburn was situated. It contained a three-piece suite and table and chairs; so it served as a sitting room cum dining room cum kitchen; consequently it was the most used room. Calico shivered as she got out of bed, picked up her clothes, and hurried downstairs to dress in front of the stove. If she was late getting up and there were people in the kitchen, Calico would put her clothes in bed with her to warm them up, and then change into them in bed. It was rather awkward, but better than feeling the freezing air on naked skin.

When her father came in to breakfast he remarked on the hard frost the previous night that had given him an extra task of breaking the thick layer of ice on the animals drinking troughs. He laughed when he recounted the ducks antics when expecting to find water they slid across the iced pond.

'Oh dear! Dad. Were they hurt, what did you do?' asked Calico concerned.

'I gave them three for presentation, and four for artistic content,' laughed her father, still maintaining a sense of humour in adversity. The farm turned into a bitter place during a hard winter; the rough had to be taken with the smooth and so it was endured. His hands and feet, more often than not, were cold. However well he wrapped up, the chill weather seemed to reach into his very bones. Outside water pipes froze up quickly, so churns of water had to be ferried from the house. Hay had to be distributed to the animals in outlying fields. The milking cows were often kept in overnight; which meant there were extra to muck out the following day.

Calico enjoyed the preparations leading up to Christmas. Her mother made the puddings and the mincemeat in September; the cake in October, which she almonded in November and iced in December. The mince pies and sausage rolls were made Christmas week. She also honey-baked a large gammon, and boiled an ox-tongue. They bought the turkey for Christmas dinner fresh from the local market. Calico's father bid for the biggest birds at the auction and as there was not much demand for them, they were knocked down at giveaway prices.

This year Calico accompanied her father to the market, to take some calves and buy the turkey; a thirty-two pound bird was successfully bid for by them. At the market the dealers were in high spirits, they always seemed cheerful to Calico. There was a lot of banter going on between them and the auctioneer, who came in for a lot of jokes at his expense. He took it in good humour, and dealt out a few cutting remarks of his own. Calico and her father were waiting, with the other farmers, for the calves to go through the auction ring. The auctioneer was called away before he started the selling. While he was absent, one of the calf-dealers commandeered his microphone. He then told a joke to the audience surrounding the calf-ring, through the microphone, which met with much laughter. The dealer passed the microphone on to the dealer next to him, who sang an Adge Cutler song. The microphone passed from one to the other. They told jokes, did impersonations, and sang songs to keep the audience amused, while they were waiting. Calico was disappointed when the auctioneer returned and ended the impromptu concert, as, judging by the deafening applause, was everybody else. Her father got a good price for his calves. Calico tried to see who bought them, but the dealers had their own imperceptible signs, known only to the auctioneer, to register their bids, so the others did not know who they were bidding against. One dealer winked his eye; one raised an eyebrow; one twitched his cheek; one moved his thumb slightly; one nodded his head; one raised his walking stick a fraction; one scratched his ear and so on. Sometimes the farmer who owned the calf would put in a bid, in an effort to raise the price. But he had to time it right or he could end up buying his own calf back.

Calico's father collected his calf money in cash from the offices of the auctioneers, situated on the premises, and paid for the turkey. He made his way back to his farm truck, chatting with several neighbouring farmers on the way. This was a meeting place, where they could swap information and gossip. Although their land might be adjoining each others, they did not come into contact often when on their respective farms, except if one wanted to borrow a piece of equipment or machinery from the other. They were usually too busy to socialise.

On arriving home they proudly showed Mother their purchase, but she was worried it would not fit in the Rayburn oven.

'That'll be all right you'll find,' assured Father, which was his usual comment on a problem. After being plucked and drawn, it was found the turkey would just fit in the oven; if it was placed on its breast and tipped forward, so the back legs were raised high. Calico's father breathed a sigh of relief, having escaped a helping of tongue pie from his wife. He would not admit it, but considerations like the size of the oven had not entered his head when buying the turkey.

On Christmas Eve day, Calico put up the decorations, and decked out the rooted Christmas tree brought in from the garden, in its finery of glittering tinsel and shiny baubles. Her father picked a trailer-load of holly, leaving it on the front lawn for anyone who wanted some. The milk lorry driver, delivery men and village people, all collected their free sprigs. Mr Brown always visited with a bunch of mistletoe in exchange for the holly he took. Her parents tried to do as much as possible towards the next day, so they could relax after the turkey meal.

On Christmas Eve Calico and her mother made up the stuffings: sage and onion, chestnut, and sausage forcemeat. They stuffed the turkey and sewed it up securely. They par-boiled the potatoes and parsnips for roasting the next day and prepared the brussel sprouts. They wound streaky bacon around chipolata sausages, leaving some bacon to cover the breast of the turkey. Infused a clove-studded onion in milk ready for the bread sauce, whilst sipping the odd glass of sherry in between. Meanwhile, Calico's father laid fires in the sitting room and the dining room, filled the brass coal scuttles and the log boxes, ready for the morning; being a special occasion these rooms were being used.

Calico's parents went to bed at their usual time, as, like any other day of the year, they had to be up early in the morning. Calico went to Midnight Mass at the local church. She had been confirmed, so she could take Communion. She remembered what Christmas was really about as she knelt in front of the altar. The arrival of God's son, Jesus Christ. It made her feel humble and ashamed of the way He had been treated, while on Earth. She doubted if His reception would be so very different, nowadays.

Churches had an effect on Calico. She was going to be kind, unselfish, keep God's commandments; which meant not seeing Charles again. She was full of good intentions while within its confines, and for a few hours after, then all these thoughts would be pushed to a corner of her mind, when she got on with living her life.

On the way home a few flakes of snow began to fall. The sky overhead was inky-black. Everything was still and quiet. Calico could hear her footfalls echoing, and by the time she reached home, they had been silenced to a scrunch by a layer of snow. She put her coat, scarf and boots in front of the Rayburn to dry them overnight. As it was gone midnight, which meant it was now Christmas Day, she felt justified in opening her presents. Most of which had been opened already at the corners, peeked into, and stuck back down again. She had one present left to come, from William. She had made the mistake of confiding to him that she could never wait until Christmas Day to find out what was in her presents. He refused to leave his present with her, saying he would bring it with him on Boxing Day. He had been invited for the day by Calico's parents on her prompting.

Calico got up Christmas morning in time to cook breakfast for her mother and father. The view out of the kitchen window could have come straight from a greeting card: a white blanket covered the landscape. The snow had ceased falling, and though Calico would have liked it to continue, she knew it made life more difficult for farmers. Her father said, as he came through the kitchen door, 'Thank goodness it's stopped. I didn't relish the thought of a lot a snow shovelling on my one day of relaxation.'

They had breakfast and Calico washed it up, while her mother went on with the dinner. She had put the turkey in the oven before she went milking. Calico pigged herself on chocolates, sweets, marshmallows, and chocolate biscuits; her excuse being, 'Well, after all, it is Christmas.'

There was a sad moment when Calico discovered her rabbit Reuben was dead. She told her father about it, her eyes shining with tears and near to spilling over. 'What a shame, we've bought a turkey now,' was his reply, trying to make her laugh. She smiled despite herself, and said, 'Oh Dad! He'd be a bit tough for dinner.' She felt the tears trickling down her cheeks. She brushed them quickly away, when she saw that Gran and Granfer had arrived for Christmas dinner. Gran told her tears were indulging in self-pity; that we did not cry for others only for ourselves. When people and animals died, we did not need to cry for them, they were in a better place than the ones they had left behind. If that was the case, thought Calico, why did she feel better after a good cry? She did not cry often, but when a tragedy befell her, or someone close to her, she could not keep the tears from flowing.

Calico laid the table for dinner. Placing a cracker by each setting. They were drinking her mother's homemade wine with the meal: gooseberry with the main course and rhubarb with the Christmas pudding and brandy sauce. Calico's parents did not drink much throughout the year. Early morning milking with a hangover was not to be recommended, the cows seemed to bellow louder, they had scant sympathy for human weaknesses.

Dinner was soon over. The turkey was now a shadow of its former self. The washing-up had been done. They were all relaxing in front of the blazing sitting room fire, staring into the hearth, watching the sparks making patterns on the sooted chimney breast. They were mesmerised by the flames licking around the logs in various hues of colour, darting in and out, dying down and then flaring up again elsewhere. Soon the peace was punctuated with snores. Only Calico and her father remained awake.

'This is the life,' her father sighed contentedly. 'Hearth and home. Food in yer belly, drink in yer hand, and roasting by a log fire. What man could ask for more? Food, drink, and warmth.'

'Are you happy, Dad?' asked Calico.

'Happy,' he thought about the word. 'No. Happy comes in flashes and doesn't linger. It's not a constant state. I'm not happy, yet I'm not unhappy, so I must be somewheres between the two, contented with my lot.'

'Do you like living here?' Calico continued, now she had got him talking.

'Yes, but I'd like living anywhere. You see, I like living. Though there are some that are loath to leave this old house,' he said mysteriously.

'What do you mean?' questioned Calico.

'Well,' began her father. 'It was the night you and mother went to the Christmas whistdrive in the village hall. I was in the kitchen looking through the *Farmers Weekly*. I heard voices in the hall, and thought you two had arrived home, though I thought it strange, because I hadn't heard the front door. Then I listened a bit harder when you didn't come through to the kitchen. I couldn't make out what was being said, but I realised they weren't your voices, these were male. I got my gun from the backhouse to go and challenge them. Those dogs of yourn were no good, they wouldn't come with me. I went into the hall; it was empty.'

Calico felt a cold chill pass through her. 'That's eerie Dad. Why didn't you mention it before?'

'I didn't want to scare you. But sat here it seems silly now. It was probably an over-active imagination,' he concluded.

Before Calico could speculate further, her mother woke up and suggested it was time for a cup of tea and a piece of Christmas cake. After this her Gran and Granfer went home. Her parents did the milking. Calico prepared some dishes for the following day, and made the base of the trifle. They ate a tea of bread, cheese, and homemade pickles, then played cards until bedtime, indulging in nuts, crisps, dates stuffed with almond paste, and drinking ginger wine.

On Boxing Day morning, Calico was met with a drift of snow outside the door, when she let the dogs out. It must have been snowing hard all night, and strong gusts of wind had heaped it up unevenly. The dogs loved the snow, and after a tentative investigation of it, they ran through it and rolled over in it.

Calico's father was not too pleased at breakfast. 'That'll teach me for being so smug yesterday,' he stated. 'He always makes us pay.'

William arrived mid-morning in his father's Land-Rover. Calico was surprised that she felt really pleased to see him. He greeted her with a hug and a kiss, which was quite demonstrative for him. She returned his kiss with more feeling than usual. He, sensing this, reciprocated. Gently he inserted his tongue between her lips. Calico thought of Charles and a thrill ran through her, the sort her body had previously reserved for Charles, damn him. Was it William's kiss or the thought of Charles that had had the effect? Their kiss was long and lingering. Reluctantly they broke apart, their eyes searching each other's face. At that moment on cue, a head protruded round the dairy door. The face of Calico's father grinned impishly, 'Thought I heard you arrive, gave you a few minutes to greet each other afore I said hello.'

The colour heightened in both their cheeks.

'My this wind must be biting to redden yer cheeks in so short a time,' chided Calico's father.

'Come inside William,' said Calico quickly, sending her father a grimace.

'Ah! Thees get on in the warm. I'll see you later,' chuckled her father.

William handed Calico a box. Inside was a gold bracelet watch. Calico thanked him, and they kissed again, in the hallway. They entered the kitchen. Calico's mother was carving the cold meats, and laying them out on a platter. She welcomed William. They were having baked potatoes and a variety of salads for accompaniment, sherry trifle, fresh cream gateau, and reheated Christmas pudding, for dessert. There was usually plenty of cream about because her parents would skim the layer of cream, that had settled on the previous night's milk, from the churns; as soon as they had received the results of the monthly milk tests. The milk was tested for quality, the solids and the percentage of fats, by the Milk Marketing Board, who paid them accordingly on the results.

The Boxing Day meal passed pleasantly, with a lot of laughter. Calico found herself liking William more and more. He kept her parents amused with his conversation, and his sense of humour matched her father's. Even though they were all aware that outside the elements were against them, and if the snow kept up there would be a hard time to come, it did not dull their spirits; they did not dwell on it or worry over it; they would take it in their stride when the need arose, which made them good company.

Snow had been falling for most of the day. Calico's mother suggested William stay the night to avoid the hazardous journey home. William thanked her, but said he couldn't stay in case the snow got a lot deeper and lasted several days. Much as he would like to spend the time with them, his father would need his help on the farm at home if the weather worsened. He left before dark, as driving in the snow was safer by natural light, than artificial light.

He promised to telephone Calico as soon as he arrived home, to let her know he was safe. Calico was worried about him driving in these conditions. When they had kissed goodbye, Calico had suddenly not wanted him to go.

She realised she did feel something for him, she did not know what. She wanted him to stay so she could find out, but she wouldn't admit it to him. So, after clinging together briefly, he took his leave of her. When he rang much later that evening, she was relieved. He had a lot of trouble getting through to his home. There were accidents and abandoned cars on most of the roads. He had to keep turning back and trying another route until eventually he had a clear run through a network of lanes.

The following day the snow was much deeper. The milking cows were being kept in their stalls all the time; the warmth from their breath and bodies melted the snow on the cowstall tiles, resulting in six-foot-long, dagger-shaped icicles hanging down from the roof. Calico's father dug out a path from the back door to the dairy, and laid ashes along it to prevent slip-ups on the ice that formed underneath. The heifers and steers were brought nearer the farm into the parrock, so it was easier to keep a watchful eye on them. The milk had to be taken out to the main road by tractor and trailer, because the milk lorry was unable to get through the lanes. Water was brought back in the empty churns from the village stand-pipe, as all the cold water pipes in the farmhouse had frozen up solid. The cows still needed plenty of water to make their milk.

A few days later, so much snow had fallen that even the tractor and trailer could not get through to the main road, the drifts were so deep in places. Several village folk came to the farm to ask for milk. Calico's father gave it away to them. 'Better they have it and make use of it, than pour it down the drain and waste it,' he said. 'The cows need to be milked, whatever.'

They melted snow in front of fires for the cows drinking water. There was a constant stream of dripping clothes around the Rayburn; exchanging wet ones for dry every time they came in. It was a miserable existence while the snow lasted. The countryside took on a fairytale appearance under its white mantle. Frosted trees sparkled in winter sunlight. The surface of drifts, still virgin, glistened. Icicles twinkled. How could the scene look so breathtakingly beautiful, and cause so much aggravation? *There must be a message in there somewhere*, thought Calico.

The villagers banded together and helped the farmers to dig a path through the drifts, so they could reach the main road for the milk lorry, the water, and to collect cow-cake from the feed merchant's lorries.

Then the slow thaw began turning the yard into a skating rink overnight. Calico's mother said it was just as well she had built-in padding, the amount of time she spent landing on her behind. Her wellies were old and had lost their tread, so she put a pair of socks over them for extra grip. The dogs got around without any trouble, their pads and nails gripping on the ice. They thought it great fun when the humans kept slipping down to their level. Everywhere looked drab, dismal, and soggy. The trees no longer looked as though they had been dipped in sugar frosting, transformed now to resemble leaky pipes, constantly drip, drip, dripping. The previous bright whiteness was now a murky grey.

William rang to wish Calico a happy New Year. She wanted so much to see him again. He must have felt the same for he told her he missed her. It must be as Duc De La Rochefoucauld said, *'L'absence diminue les médiocres passions, et augmente les grandes, comme le vent éteint les bougies, et allume le feu*. ('Absence diminishes commonplace passions and increases great ones, as the wind extinguishes candles, and kindles fires.') William said the snow was fading fast where he lived. Calico agreed the same was happening where she was too, so they arranged to meet the next day but one, which was a Saturday. It was Calico's last night at home, for she had to be back at the Mansion House on Sunday evening.

William and Calico did not have long together. By the time William and her father had discussed the past week's events, and how each other had managed on their farms, time was moving on. When Calico's parents had gone to bed leaving them alone in the kitchen, William seized Calico and kissed her straight away. 'I've been wanting to do that all evening.' Calico said nothing, remembering the last time she had heard that remark. It was from Charles's lips, when they had garaged the Daimler. Was he always going to haunt her? How could she know how she felt about William, if Charles was still in her system, and the memory of him was always prevalent?

'I've missed you. It was awful knowing you were only a matter of miles away, and I wasn't able to visit you,' continued William. Still getting no response from Calico, he carried on, 'I think a lot about you Calico. Do you feel the same way?'

'I like you a lot,' replied Calico, truthfully.

'Would you get engaged? I've never found anyone I've wanted to ask before,' said William, tentatively.

'Oh William!' exclaimed Calico confused. 'I don't know. It's rather sudden. We haven't known each other long.'

'You don't have to know someone for long to know that this is it: here is a person I could spend the rest of my life with; I felt that the first time I saw you,' answered William with conviction.

Calico was flattered. 'Can I consider for a while?'

'Of course,' replied William, smiling. 'At least you haven't turned me down straight away. And if you are willing to consider it you may even say yes, and make me very happy.'

Why did men do this, wondered Calico. Emotional blackmail. Making you feel guilty, as if their future happiness depended on you, was entirely in your hands. The worst thing in the world to be blessed with is a conscience, and Calico had more than her fair share meted out to her.

'William,' she began. 'Now that you've asked me to get engaged, and I've agreed to think about it. Will you not dwell on it or refer to it again, and I'll give you my answer in due course?'

'If that's what you want,' he said, shrugging his shoulders.

'It is,' Calico replied firmly.

Chapter Twelve

Amy's Anguish

When Calico returned to the Mansion House on Sunday evening, Amy was already there, looking even worse. She was much thinner, her uniform hung on her and her sallow skin was taut over her face, accentuating her sunken eyes. Calico was shocked. She could almost visualise the outline of the skull beneath this death mask that presented itself as Amy. She felt helpless in another's trouble. She spoke matter-of-factly to Amy; though wanting to know why she had deteriorated so rapidly, instead she said, 'Did you have a good Christmas with your mother?'

'No,' said Amy sadly. 'I stayed at her flat. She had an offer to do a pantomime at the last minute. It was up north. So when I arrived home, I found a note on the kitchen table to say she would be away for the Christmas and New Year.'

'I wish I'd known,' said Calico feeling sorry for Amy, the tears welling up in her eyes. 'You could have spent Christmas with me.'

Calico realised how lucky she was to have parents that cared. They were not demonstrative, but she knew they were always there for her, and each other. Ordinary country folk satisfied with their lot, and not striving for fame or fortune. Tryphena's parents were wealthy and well-connected and Amy's parent was talented, creative, and might one day be famous, but at what cost to their children. Tryphena was hard, bitter, and mistrustful of affection: Amy was hurt, bewildered, and desperate for affection. The present situation that both found themselves in could be traced back to their childhood; the period in life that shapes us for the future.

'Once inside the flat, I couldn't bring myself to venture out,' said Amy opening up a little.

'Didn't you go out for food?' questioned Calico.

'No. I ate the odd few things Mother had left in the storecupboard when I was hungry; which wasn't often,' answered Amy.

'Why didn't you give me a ring?' demanded Calico.

'The phone wasn't working. I think Mother hasn't paid the phone bill, she's not well-off,' Amy admitted.

'What did you do all the time?'

'Watched telly, listened to music, tried to read books but I couldn't concentrate for long. Mother had bought a lot of drink in ready for Christmas, hoping friends would visit. I drank that most of the time.'

Her mother had money to buy drink, but not to pay the phone bill, thought Calico. *No wonder Amy looks like she does: not eating properly; an excess of alcohol; probably not sleeping well.* After the ordeal she had been through, she needed looking after, not to be left alone to dwell on it.

'I feel quite hungry. Let's go and make some scrambled eggs,' suggested Calico brightly, hoping Amy would agree, she needed nourishment.

'I'm not really hungry,' began Amy.

'Well, just try a little then,' interrupted Calico determined to make her eat something. Thinking that if she began to eat, gradually it would start to build her up again. Calico was unaware of the other reason why Amy was in such a state.

They went downstairs to the kitchen. Calico persuaded Amy to eat some scrambled egg but she refused the toast. She also managed to encourage Amy to drink a milky cup of Horlicks. Tomorrow morning she would try her with a cup of Ovaltine, and get her to drink Lucozade. *It will take time before Amy can face a main meal*, thought Calico, *but if I can fill her up with eggs, milk, cheese, and get some vitamins and minerals into her; it will help counteract some of the damage the alcohol has done to her.*

All the staff on their return the next day were worried about Amy, with the exception of Mr Rolph, who said that if she did not 'shape up' he would be forced to let her go, her appearance was not up to the standard required as a representative of the Mansion House. He would give her two weeks to improve herself. What swines some men were, thought Calico. There were the two who were responsible for Amy's present plight, and now Mr Rolph capitalising on the situation, to enable him to get rid of her. He had never forgiven Amy and Calico for upsetting Sophia. It had taken him ages to get her favours back, not to mention the gifts he had to ply her with in the meantime, before she relented.

Mr Rolph's remarks left Amy more upset than ever. The Mansion House was the one stable thing left in her existence. Her work was a reason to rise in the morning. The people here were like the family she had never known. She enjoyed the chatter around the kitchen table at break, and the dining table at lunchtime. Though she did not join in the conversations any more, they meant that life was still going on around her. She liked to hear Cook talk about the Royal Family, her sister, and the neighbours in the surrounding flats. She enjoyed listening to Susan berate about her husband and his exploits: how he looked through pornographic magazines at naked women, when she was pregnant, which upset her, how he was so insensitive towards her, making her feel sexually unattractive and unwanted. The nude calendar he had on his workshop wall was, she felt, a betrayal. Why did he want to look at pictures of other naked women posing in different positions; wasn't she all he wanted? Apparently not. She found out he was having an affair with a canteen assistant at his works. Everyone sympathised and suffered along with her until it was over. Then there was Maria; they had all agonised with her as she took test after test at the infertility clinic, and awaited the results with as much anguish as she did herself. Grace was given all sorts of advice by the others on how to deal with her brute of a drunken husband, because they worried about her safety. Grace listened to them, knowing they were well-meant, but never acting on any of their advice. He had not always been like this, it was only since he had been made redundant. When he found another job Grace was sure he would return to being the husband and father he used to be; she tried to explain this to the others.

They also noticed how weary Vera often looked. Her aged mother had kept her up again most of the night; she had wet the bed twice. They tried to persuade Vera to put her mother in a nursing home but Vera could not do it. She said she would feel guilty, as if she were handing over her responsibility to others. Besides, she reasoned, her mother must have been up in the night with her, when she was a baby and she hadn't sent her away for being a nuisance, and keeping her awake.

If Amy had to quit the Mansion House, then there was nothing left for her. She was in no fit condition to go for job interviews. She needed to stay there among friends in familiar surroundings. She was safe there. Food, warmth and a bed were provided. She did not want to go out and face the rest of the world. She thought she would be able to stay there forever. If she was denied this sanctuary, what would she do?

Amy did not appear for work the following morning. It was Sophia's day off. Calico coped on her own, thinking a few hours extra sleep would do Amy good; Cook agreed with her. Calico went upstairs to wake Amy before Mr Rolph came in so she would not get into trouble with him. Calico could get no answer to her knocks on Amy's door. She could not knock any louder or Sophia might awaken, and come to find out what all the noise was about. So Calico finding the door unlocked, opened it and entered Amy's bedroom. She tried to rouse her, but failed. Then she noticed the empty bottle of tablets on the bedside table. Without stopping to notify Mr Rolph, who had by now arrived, she rang for an ambulance. She went back to Amy, and tried to shake her awake.

Mr Rolph sent Susan upstairs to find out why the duty parlourmaids were not in the kitchen, and that he wanted to see them immediately.

'Oh no!' exclaimed Susan, when Calico informed her of her fears. 'An overdose. Quick get her out of bed, we have to keep her moving.'

Vera joined them, having been sent by Mr Rolph to discover why no one had appeared in answer to his summons, with the message that if they did not appear before him within five minutes, he would give them a written warning.

'Asso to him,' retorted Calico uncharacteristically. 'Amy is more important than his pompous threats. Will you take a message back to him. Tell him we are unavoidably detained, and can he direct the ambulance men up here when they arrive.'

'Right you are,' answered Vera. 'But he's going to be very annoyed with you.'

'So what's new? He's devoted his life to going about causing misery to others, when he doesn't get his own way,' snapped Calico.

Vera departed, not looking forward to relaying Calico's words to Mr Rolph. All the staff, excepting Maria and Sophia, disliked him. He had a sneering way and treated them rudely. Expecting complete obedience from them, Mr Rolph went into a rage, that Calico had had the audacity, the effrontery, to send an order to him. Full of his own self-importance, he never even inquired who the ambulance was for. Vera made a hasty exit, in case he reverted to the customs of ancient Roman times and punished the messenger for the message, leaving him muttering to himself. She told Cook about Amy. Cook took it upon herself to send Vera out to wait for the ambulance. She suggested it would be better if they came through the staff entrance and up the backstairs. She gave Vera a colander full of sprouts saying, 'If Mr Rolph asks where you are, I'll tell him you've gone to fetch me some sprouts from the gardener.'

Calico and Susan were still trying to revive Amy. 'I didn't think she'd let that break-up with her boyfriend affect her so. I mean they weren't going together that long. Men, nothing but trouble. Break your heart, then go on to the next, like my old man. Damned if I'd do away with myself over him though. Wouldn't give him the satisfaction, rather stay around and annoy the blighter,' rambled Susan. Calico could not tell Susan why Amy was so unhappy and upset, as her friend had told her sub rosa; she could only agree it was Amy's boyfriend who was the catalyst.

The ambulancemen arrived and quickly and efficiently dealt with Amy. Taking her down the backstairs, as requested by Cook, so it would not come to the Lord Mayor's attention, if it could be possibly avoided. Now that Amy had been transported off to the best place for her, Calico had to face Mr Rolph. She stood before him defiant.

'Well, what have you got to say in your defence?' demanded Mr Rolph menacingly.

'Nothing,' retorted Calico, not wanting to tell him about Amy's attempted suicide bid.

'Nothing, nothing?' repeated Mr Rolph, his voice rising in pitch. 'You had plenty to say just now. Treating me as an underling. How dare *you* send orders.' His face contorted with rage. He spat out the next words venomously, 'To me, me.'

Calico braced herself, she thought he was going to hit her. She had never seen anyone in such a temper. His eyes gleamed wildly and his lips worked feverishly, as he tried to control himself. 'You will be sorry my girl. I'm giving you a week's notice and no references. If you cross me again in the meantime, it will be instant dismissal. The same goes for your stupid friend. I suppose she thought she would gain my sympathy with this latest stunt of hers. She does not fool me pretending she's ill.'

Calico looked at him aghast. What a frightful inhuman person; what was he saying?

'Now get out of my sight,' he ordered.

Calico had no hesitation, she obeyed. She could not bear to look on him any more. She was being dismissed. Her first proper job, and she had been given the sack. Her crime was helping a fellow human being in trouble. What a world this was, it seemed the cruel and unjust, the selfish and dishonest, time and again came out on top. *Talk about the meek shall inherit the earth; by the time these sort of people have finished with it, the earth will not be worth inheriting*, thought Calico, as she went upstairs to change.

Cook stopped Calico on her way out through the kitchen. 'Where are you going?' she questioned.

'To the hospital, to be with Amy,' answered Calico.

'But you're supposed to be on duty. Mr Rolph won't be pleased when he finds out. You can't do any good going there. It'll be a while before the doctors can tell you anything. Why not wait until you're off duty at lunchtime. You can ring the hospital at breaktime for news,' cajoled Cook.

'No. I'm going now,' retorted Calico adamantly. 'I don't care what Mr Rolph thinks; he's given me a week's notice anyway. I want to be there when Amy pulls through. I want her to know someone cares, that someone wants her to live.' And she proceeded to tell Cook about the miserable Christmas Amy spent on her own.

'You're right, Amy needs someone with her when she comes to,' agreed Cook. 'I'll come to the hospital as soon as I finish here. I'll bring as many of the staff as I can muster. Amy needs to know she has friends who care what happens to her.'

At breaktime Calico's absence was noted by Mr Rolph. 'And where is Calico?' he asked nastily.

'Doing an errand for me,' put in Cook quickly.

'And what would that be, an errand of mercy, visiting the sick perhaps?' he returned sarcastically.

'I broke the grapefruit knife this morning,' answered Cook. 'I sent her into town to buy a new one.'

'Let me see the broken knife,' he demanded.

'I threw it in the rubbish bin,' retorted Cook.

'How convenient being dustbin collection day,' he sneered. 'Why did you not tell me. I would have ordered you a grapefruit knife from our suppliers.'

'I need it for tomorrow morning,' replied Cook. 'It would take several days delivery from them.'

'What about paying for it? You didn't come to me for petty cash,' he queried.

'I couldn't find you so I took the money out of my own purse,' parried Cook.

'I will just check to make sure the other knives are intact. You seem to be getting careless with Mansion House property,' he said walking across to the cutlery drawer. The other staff held their breath. The calm before the storm; any minute now he would erupt, when he found the grapefruit knife there. Poor Cook, their hearts went out to her.

'Everything seems satisfactory,' Mr Rolph said turning to Cook. There was an audible sigh of relief from the staff. Cook smiled sweetly, with her hand on the overall pocket which contained the grapefruit knife. She would have to buy a new one on her way to the hospital. Mr Rolph would expect a receipt and a brand new knife.

The others kept silent about the incident, and changed the subject quickly as Maria and Sophia were present. Although it was Sophia's day off, she still joined the rest of the staff at breaktimes and for her meals, having nowhere else to go.

'The police still haven't solved who stole the silver,' announced Vera. 'Apparently they are going to question all the staff again, in case they missed something the first time.'

'I thought Jane's boyfriend was the culprit,' interceded Grace.

'Seems not. He had a cast-iron alibi. He was working in Scotland that week,' explained Vera.

'They haven't questioned me yet,' stated the gardener. 'I went home at lunchtime on the day they found out it was missing, and had the next few days as holiday.'

'The police must have been confident they'd caught the thief, and stopped their line of questioning,' suggested Cook.

'I can't remember what I said in my statement,' admitted Susan, worried.

'It doesn't matter,' consoled Cook. 'If you told the truth then, and you tell the truth this time, they won't differ. Unless of course you took the silver out in your knickers each day.'

'That's not very likely,' snapped back Susan.

'Only joking,' said Cook taken aback by her reaction.

'I know, but I don't wear any knickers,' laughed Susan. They all laughed loudly at this, except Sophia and Maria, whose command of the English language was not sufficient to recognise humour. The two, feeling out of it, left the table, and could be heard babbling away as they mounted the stairs.

Cook then gained the remaining staff's attention. She repeated to them what Calico had told her regarding Amy and her thoughtless mother at Christmas time. She implored them to join her in visiting Amy that afternoon. 'We should unite in a show of strength. Let her see she has friends who care about her.'

'I'll come,' volunteered Vera. 'I'll ring home and ask the sitter to stay a few extra hours with Mother.'

'Me too,' agreed Susan. 'I'll get a friend to meet the children from school and give them tea.'

'I expect I'll get into trouble with the old man, but that's too bad. Amy needs me more than he does,' said Grace, with a glimpse of the spirit she used to have before she got married and had it broken.

'I'll be there, and the wife. I know she'll agree when I tell her,' said the gardener, and added, 'I'll let Charles know.'

'Thanks, I knew you wouldn't let me down. Everyone's born with the milk of human kindness in them; some only have an eggcupful, but you lot have it in bucketfuls,' said Cook, pleased. 'And now back to work. We'll not mention it again, lest the wicked stepmother and the two ugly sisters are ear-wigging. I'll see you all at the hospital. Oh! I forgot, I'm ringing the hospital later to see how Amy's progressing. When you come into the kitchen raise your eyebrows at me. If it's good news I'll give you the thumbs up; if it's bad news I'll give you the thumbs down. I don't want Mr Rolph to know, he thinks Amy was taken to hospital because she's pretending to be ill, and then she can get sick leave. He doesn't know she tried to commit suicide.'

They all went back to work. While Mr Rolph was upstairs attending to the Lord Mayor, Cook rang the hospital. All they would divulge was that Amy's condition was satisfactory. Well at least she was still alive; to Cook that represented good news. It was a happier crew that gathered at lunchtime. Cook opened a bottle of wine to celebrate. Maria wanted to know why they were having wine with their meal today.

'It's my cat's birthday,' offered Cook by way of explanation. Maria looked puzzled, but questioned her no further. She loved wine, if she continued talking she would miss valuable drinking time so any excuse would do, she thought, as she topped her glass up again and wished Tiddles many more birthdays.

Amy was so pleased to see everyone. They brought her flowers, fruit, chocolates and magazines. She cried. They thought she was still upset; but it was their kindness and show of affection that moved her to tears. They chatted to her animatedly, keeping the conversation away from her suicide attempt. They told her about the police wanting to question them all again.

'It's funny,' commented the gardener looking perplexed. 'I dug over the ground by the laurel hedge that morning before breaktime, and I didn't see no silver sugar tongs. Must get myself a pair of specs, instead of using yours Mother,' he said to his wife.

When they had all departed, except for Calico, Amy started to cry again.

'Don't cry Amy. Doesn't it make you feel better knowing you have so many good friends?'

'No,' answered Amy. 'It's because they are so kind to me, that it makes me feel worse.'

'I don't understand,' said Calico, a little impatient with her friend seeming ungrateful when everyone had made so much effort to visit her.

'Oh Calico! I don't know what to do,' wailed Amy. 'I think I'm pregnant.'

Calico shut her eyes and covered her face with her hands. *Poor Amy*, she thought, *is there to be no end to her troubles?* 'The doctor told you?' she asked.

'No, I haven't seen a doctor,' admitted Amy. 'But I'm three weeks late, my period is always regular.'

'It could be the shock of the assault on you, or not eating properly. There are all sorts of reasons why it could be that late or missed altogether,' reasoned Calico, trying to pacify her.

'I'm pregnant. I know I am. I couldn't go through with an abortion, and I didn't want it inside me for nine months reminding me of that awful day. So I decided to take the easy way out, but fate was against me in that. I'm still here having to face this problem,' sobbed Amy.

'You may not have a problem. Wait until you see a doctor, and it's been confirmed. Then we'll work something out,' said Calico confidently, though not sure herself what they would do if Amy was pregnant. Amy agreed to have a word with the duty doctor when he came on his round of the ward. Calico left her when the doctor appeared at the door of the ward, hoping fervently that a test would prove negative.

On the way out Calico noticed a blonde-haired woman talking to the receptionist. She was heavily made-up in an effort to counteract her fading beauty. Her voice was loud and carrying. 'I must see my baby; how is she, poor lamb? I've just heard about it from a neighbour.' She turned to the short, fat, balding man who accompanied her. 'Wait here a moment darling, I won't be long. I just want to make sure she's all right and then we can go out to dinner.'

Calico had an awful feeling that 'that' was Amy's mother. Oh well! At least she had turned up eventually to see her.

It was late when Calico arrived back at the Mansion House. The house seemed strangely silent. No Sophia glued to the television. Everywhere downstairs was in darkness. Calico went straight up to her room. It had been a long tiring day, all she wanted was sleep.

Chapter Thirteen

Who is the Thief?

The under-butler was sat at the kitchen table waiting for Calico. He was a kind, gentle, man with a rotund Pickwickian figure. This morning he looked distressed; his eyes had lost their usual twinkle. 'Mr Jukes!' exclaimed Calico surprised to see him. 'What are you doing here so early; couldn't you sleep?'

'I've come to give you a hand. Sophia won't be on duty this morning, and as Amy is in hospital, that leaves you on your own,' explained Mr Jukes.

'I see,' said Calico, not letting on that she had managed by herself more than once.

'You'll have to instruct me. I've never been a parlourmaid before,' he continued, trying to make light of the situation.

'Where's Sophia?' asked Calico.

'I'll tell you later, when all the staff are present,' he answered mysteriously. 'Now which pinny do I use for morning wear?'

Calico laughed, 'I don't think they're your size.'

The serving of the Lord Mayor and the consort's breakfast went without a hitch. A remark directed at Mr Jukes by the Mayor left Calico wondering. 'Heard anything more?'

'No,' replied Mr Jukes.

'Nasty business that, leaves an unpleasant taste in the mouth,' commented the Mayor in a haughty tone.

Mr Jukes called a staff meeting when all the full-time workers had arrived; Tryphena excluded. 'I've brought you all together,' began Mr Jukes, 'because I have to inform you of a rather delicate matter. I wanted you all to hear it at the same time so that you all get the same version; I know what happens when people hear different bits of a story, and it gets blown out of all proportion. What I am going to say must remain within these four walls for the time being. Is that understood?'

Everyone nodded assent. Susan whispered to Calico, 'What an old wind-bag, why doesn't he get to the point, leave the groundwork and start dishing out the dirt.'

'The reason Mr Rolph, Sophia, and Maria are not with us today,' he continued, 'is because they have been taken to the police station for questioning. Also Mr Rolph's son. This does not mean they are guilty of stealing the silver; no charges have been brought against them at the moment. I suggest you keep an open mind on the matter.'

Smiles broke out around the room.

'Of course the butler did it,' exclaimed Vera. 'He always does in the books I read.'

'It could well have been an inside job,' put in the gardener thoughtfully. 'I dug around the laurels that morning and the silver tongs weren't there then. Charles found them during our morning break. It doesn't take a Sherlock Holmes to figure out the approximate time they were dropped there. It wasn't the night before as we were led to believe.'

'That's right,' interrupted Cook. 'Who picked up extra laundry baskets and didn't stay long at breaktime; whereas usually we can't get rid of him?'

'Mr Rolph's son, of course,' answered Susan.

'Correct,' said Cook triumphantly. 'It all fits into place. No one would think to connect the butler's son to the stolen silver, as he was here on legitimate business.'

'Instead it was monkey business,' said Charles as he entered the room. They all focused their attention towards him.

'What have you heard?' enquired Mr Jukes. 'I know you have a network of contacts.'

'The information came through a reliable source, and was passed on to me by the judge's chauffeur,' disclosed Charles, and he proceeded to relate what he knew. 'Mr Rolph retires soon. His wife's an invalid, he doesn't say much about her. When he retires from here, he would not be able to keep seeing Sophia. He was getting the money together to buy a small hotel in Italy for himself, his wife, his son, Maria, and Sophia, so he could still keep his bit on the side going. His son was smuggling the silver out in the laundry baskets, a little every week. They thought by the time the theft was found out, they would be ensconced in their hotel in Italy.'

'I feel awful about this!' exclaimed Mr Jukes. 'I should have been more astute and realised what was going on around me.'

'It's not your fault,' assured Calico. 'You've got a trusting nature. You wouldn't dream of suspecting any of the staff of stealing, let alone such an upstanding figure as your immediate boss.'

'I must admit I thought he was beyond reproach, being a naval man who had fought for his country,' said Mr Jukes clearly upset. 'I did not even know anything untoward was going on between Mr Rolph and Sophia. I must seem a bit of an ostrich.'

'And we wouldn't have you any other way,' declared Cook. 'Will it be in the papers do you think?'

'No,' said Charles emphatically. 'It won't even get into court.'

'Haven't the police got enough evidence?' asked Vera.

'It's not that,' answered Charles. 'The police realised the robbery couldn't have taken place during the weekend the house was empty because our gardener in his statement said the silver sugar tongs weren't in the laurel hedge before breaktime. They questioned Mr Rolph's son again, because his movements fitted in with the approximate time the theft took place. They asked him if he had noticed the sugar tongs when he put the laundry baskets into the back of his van, which he always parked by the laurel hedge. His answers were not satisfactory, so they questioned several of the staff again. They found out Mr Rolph reported his lost set of keys after the silver had been handed in which was suspicious: somehow he must have heard about the find.'

'I'm the guilty one,' interrupted Cook. 'You told me about the tongs, and I told Mr Rolph.'

'And he tried to cover his tracks,' continued Charles, 'by inventing the story of his missing spare set of keys, so the police would be thrown off the scent. While they were all at the police station last night, the police searched their houses and garages. Eventually they found most of the silverware in Mr Rolph's holiday caravan near the coast.'

'Why won't they be charged then?' demanded Grace. 'Because Mr Rolph knows too much about the Council House and its goings on,' explained Charles. 'It would be an embarrassment to them all if everything came to light.'

'He gets off scot-free,' complained Susan indignantly.

'Not quite,' replied Charles. 'He loses his pension from the City Council, which would have been a tidy sum. He will be instantly dismissed from the Mansion House, as will Sophia and Maria. The police have recovered nearly all of the silverware, so he hasn't any money salted away from that either. He will find himself rather poor from now on.'

'My heart bleeds for him,' said Grace sarcastically.

'I still think he's got off light,' said the gardener.

'Me too,' agreed Susan scornfully. 'When I think what a lecherous old sod he was; how we had to be pleasant to him to keep our jobs, it makes my blood boil.'

'Sanctimonious swine,' put in Vera heatedly.

'Does this mean Amy and me won't have to leave?' enquired Calico of Mr Jukes.

'Leave, what do you mean?' he said astonished.

'Mr Rolph gave us both a week's notice.'

'Why was that?' asked Mr Jukes.

'Because I didn't report to him in person downstairs, and sent a message instead,' answered Calico.

'Surely that notice is void now?' said Charles coming to Calico's assistance. He didn't want her to leave, he hadn't finished with her yet. The others pleaded for them also.

'Of course,' affirmed Mr Jukes. 'Consider yourselves reinstated. I'll destroy the paperwork if there is any, but I expect Mr Rolph didn't make an official note of it.'

'Thank you,' said Calico relieved. 'And I know Amy will be grateful. I haven't told her yet that Mr Rolph had given her notice. I was going to wait until her health improved.'

'I think I had better break up this meeting or no work will be done this morning,' stated Mr Jukes.

There was a lot of chattering as the staff proceeded towards the door. 'I know Mr Rolph was an unpleasant man, but he was smart,' commented Cook. 'I find it hard to believe he would do such a daft thing as steal from here.'

'Love makes fools of us all,' said Susan wistfully.

'More like lust where he's concerned,' retorted Grace.

Charles hung back trying to catch Calico's eye. She had been avoiding him, and she never said goodbye to him before the Christmas holiday. He had bought her a present, a thin gold chain; but he did not get the chance to give it to her. It was no good, she was not going to acknowledge his existence. 'Calico,' he said loudly to get her attention. She stopped, he approached her. 'How is Amy?' he asked to start the conversation, while there were people still milling about the room.

'She's getting better, thank you,' answered Calico, coolly polite with him.

'That's good. I was sorry to hear about it, she's a nice kid,' he said moving closer and lowering his voice. 'I had a miserable Christmas without you. I nearly rang you at home, just to hear your voice; I found the number in the book, but I never seemed to be alone for long. I thought about you a lot, you didn't say goodbye. When can we meet again? I want to give you your Christmas present, I didn't get a chance before. Will you come out with me Friday? I've got the night off.'

'Sorry I'll be visiting Amy,' replied Calico.

'I'll pick you up from the hospital then,' he said rather presumptuously.

'I don't know how long I'll be, it could be any time,' said Calico, avoiding an outright no.

'Please, I must see you. We can arrange a definite time. As I'm not working, any time you say is fine by me,' he persuaded.

'But not by me,' returned Calico quietly.

Just then Mr Jukes entered the room.

'Ah! Calico, there you are!' he exclaimed. 'I can't find any reference to your notice in Mr Rolph's office. I suggest we don't mention it again, and you and Amy still have clean slates.'

'Right Mr Jukes, thank you very much,' said Calico, seizing her chance to make a quick exit. Leaving Charles to stare wistfully after her.

Calico joined Tryphena in her room at lunchtime. They dined on crusty bread and paté. Tryphena opened a bottle of wine. Calico was on duty that afternoon, she had one glass of wine, but declined a second. When Calico imparted the information concerning Mr Rolph and company to Tryphena, she was surprised to find she already knew.

'Several of my clients are in the law enforcement business,' stated Tryphena. 'They let slip all sorts of interesting info; I could write a book about them all. I could call it, *Confessions in the Chambers*. How's that for ambiguity?' Seeing Calico's puzzled frown Tryphena proceeded to enlighten her. 'The play on the word chambers, several meanings. Chambers could be a judge's room, some of my clients being judges; also a bedroom, where most of my work is carried out: or a torture chamber, where they thrill to the brutal caress of my whip, shudder under my studded leathers and spiked heels, and struggle excitedly against their tightening bonds fighting for breath as they climax on a wave of pain and ecstasy.'

'Sounds like a chamber of horrors to me,' said Calico appalled.

'It's that too,' agreed Tryphena. 'Then there's the Chamber of Commerce, the council chambers, see what I mean?'

'Yes, but do you think people would want to read about that sort of thing?' said Calico naively.

'Absolutely,' retorted Tryphena. 'You only have to read some of the newspapers to realise, MY SORDID NIGHT OF PASSION sells more papers than HAPPY ENDING FOR TRAGIC COUPLE.' She opened another bottle of wine and refilled her glass.

Tryphena was such a realist, thought Calico, there was no hazy glow surrounding her world. Calico tried to think the best of people but several she had come up against already had undermined the foundation of her thinking. The more she talked with Tryphena, the more her safe sunny world seemed to collapse around her. She had known nothing of these things this time last year, at home on the farm. Now she had come across rape, prostitution, theft, seducers, lechers, people who enjoyed pain, men who beat their wives, men who were unfaithful to their wives. She held on to the fact that along with this motley assortment there were also people like her father, her mother, William, Amy, Mr Jukes, Cook, Vera, Grace, the gardener, his wife, Susan, Gran, Granfer, all the village people back home; hopefully they were in the majority.

'Are you listening?' demanded Tryphena.

'Sorry, no, I was thinking,' apologised Calico. 'What did you say?'

'I said I'll be leaving soon.'

'Don't you like it here any more?' queried Calico.

'It's not my decision. The Lord Mayor's term of office is up soon. The incoming Lord Mayor doesn't require my services, he's also a bit of a prude, so I have to move from here. The City Council have provided me with a house to continue to meet their requirements. It'll be less travelling for me. They're going to fit it out with all the equipment I need. Apparently it's got cellars, which will come in useful; they're going to soundproof them. You will come to visit me?' requested Tryphena.

'I don't think so,' replied Calico feeling awkward.

'There won't be clients there all the time,' said Tryphena. 'I'll get some time off.'

'I'll meet you somewhere else,' suggested Calico. 'I'd rather not come to the house, I wouldn't feel comfortable being there.'

'That's what I like about you,' laughed Tryphena. 'You're so tender-hearted you don't like to think of those poor men suffering, yet they pay me to make them suffer, they enjoy it. I'm being kind to them by giving them what they crave. You can't understand that, can you? You expect everyone to be normal, to have straight sex in the missionary position with the one they love, to beget children. At least with masochists no one else but themselves get hurt. Unlike sadists and rapists.'

After what she had seen Amy go through, Calico could identify with that last statement. 'Yes, I agree with what you say,' she said. 'I've had my eyes opened since I left home, and I'm finding it difficult to come to terms with all the things that have happened around me or to me.'

'It's a shame. I can see you vainly struggling to hang on to your ideals and principles, while all around you people are trying to wrestle them from your grasp. You stick to them Calico,' said Tryphena emphatically. 'It's too late for me, I fell by the wayside a long time ago. Don't give in to Charles; I did, but then we use each other.'

Calico was stunned into silence. *She said don't give in to Charles*, thought Calico, *she knows; how does she know? He must have told her*. 'H-how do you know about Charles and me?' Calico stammered at last.

'There isn't much I don't know,' said Tryphena carelessly, her voice slightly slurred. 'Most people have loose tongues. I keep my eyes open and my ears tuned. Who knows when I may need the information I gather. I have enemies as well as friends among my associates. I have to collect insurance policies to keep them at bay. That's why I say, stay as sweet as you are Calico. Don't let yourself get drawn into the cut-throat twilight world; you stay out in the sunshine.' Tryphena waved her glass of wine at Calico. 'You enjoy the sweet smelling clean air that's free. Don't get dragged down into the stale-smelling foul air that you pay for with the rest of your life. You marry a nice steady lad from back home that loves you, have children, live happily ever after, quiet and content. Leave the high life and excitement for those of us who are already enmeshed in it.'

Calico was amazed. She had never heard Tryphena talk like this, but then she had never seen her drink so much before. Calico had assumed Tryphena enjoyed her life; the money, the fast cars, the expensive clothes, the rich boyfriends, the weekends away in Europe, the exotic holiday locations.

'I have to be going,' said Calico, not wanting to leave Tryphena in this state, but she was already late for the afternoon shift. 'Will you be all right?'

'Don't worry about me. Tough as old boots,' answered Tryphena, as the tears trickled down her cheeks in little black rivulets; they had been building up above her eyeliner and it had stained them. 'Oh Calico,' she sniffed. 'You will keep in contact when I leave. You're the only genuine person I know. You don't hide behind a façade that's been cultivated for years, until the person behind it believes it to be their real self, or lives in fear that one day it will be stripped away to reveal the shallow character beneath.'

'I won't desert you,' promised Calico as she left Tryphena opening another bottle of wine.

The afternoon shift was quiet. Often there was nobody else about. All the other staff went home after lunch if the Lord Mayor was out at an all day function. Calico was only there to answer the telephone or the door. She sat in the staff sitting room and read a book. Mr Jukes said he would stand in for her for the evening shift, seeing as she had been on duty since seven this morning, and he knew she wanted to visit Amy at the hospital.

Calico went upstairs to get ready to go out. She knocked on the door of Tryphena's room. There was no answer. She tried the door and it opened. She entered the room. Tryphena was fast asleep in the chair. Calico's heart plummeted as she remembered finding Amy looking the same. She looked around for empty pill bottles, there was no sign of any; it must have been the drink that put her out so soundly. The fire had died out and the room was getting chilly. Calico gently threw the bed covering over Tryphena, leaving her sleeping peacefully.

Calico arrived at Amy's bedside. 'I've been worrying about you all day. I had to work the morning and the afternoon shift, because there was no one else to cover it,' said Calico.

'Where's Soppy?' asked Amy.

Calico told her all about Mr Rolph, his son, Maria and Sophia. She also told her that Mr Rolph had given them both a week's notice. But as he had now been given instant dismissal himself by the City Council, Mr Jukes had rescinded it for them.

'What a relief!' exclaimed Amy. 'The doctor said I could leave the hospital tomorrow. I've been lying here worrying what to do. I didn't like the idea of going back to the Mansion House to face Rolphie. Mother called in to see me. When she found out I was all right, she told me she was going on holiday and then moving in with her new boyfriend, so the flat would be empty if I went there. You've made me feel better already with that piece of news. I can come back to the Mansion House. Fancy that, Rolphie and Soppy both gone. It must be a pleasure to work there now.'

'You do sound better,' encouraged Calico. 'You're not pregnant then I take it, or you wouldn't be smiling so brightly.'

'I don't know,' admitted Amy. 'I forgot about myself for the moment in thinking that Rolphie and Soppy had finally got their comeuppance.'

'Didn't you ask the doctor to take a test?' persevered Calico.

'No, I couldn't. I don't want to know. If I am, I'll have to face up to it. I'm not ready to do that yet,' said Amy sullenly.

'But it isn't going to go away if you are, just because you don't want to think about it,' insisted Calico.

'I know that,' agreed Amy. 'I'll see my own doctor when I'm back at the Mansion House. I'll be stronger to deal with it then, among friends.'

'If you are, I think we ought to tell Tryphena,' suggested Calico. 'She has a lot of contacts; she may be able to help.'

'I don't know,' said Amy evasively. 'Maybe we'll see.'

The visitors' bell rang. After a few more moments Calico took her leave of Amy.

Calico walked across the hospital car park towards the main gate. A car's lights flashed as she passed it. She heard its engine start up and it moved slowly out of its parking place and drew alongside of her. She prepared herself, stirring up her fight or flight impulses ready for action.

'Calico, hey, Calico. I've been waiting ages for you,' said the sound of a familiar voice.

'I didn't ask you to,' she retorted coldly.

'Come on, get in. It's a darn sight warmer and safer in here, than out there.'

'That's only your opinion, Charles,' snapped Calico.

'Aw come on, Calico, please,' he whined.

'I'll get in the car on two conditions,' bargained Calico.

'Anything, just name them,' said Charles relieved.

'I sit in the back, and you take me straight to the Mansion House,' demanded Calico.

'All right it's a deal,' agreed Charles grudgingly.

Calico got into the back of the car. She sat there smiling determinedly, saying to herself, *I am not falling for his charms this time. I am not special to him, only a conquest, one of many like Jane and Tryphena. How stupid I have been believing his sugar-coated words, his endearments, his practised phrases. He is nothing but a chauvinistic, egotistical, womanising bastard* (the latter was not a word Calico would use out loud, only under her breath). *But what does that make me? I nearly fell for his line and got hooked, reeled in, and laid out on a plate for him.*

Charles stopped the car a little way up the road from the Mansion House. 'Can I join you?' he asked Calico.

'No, you stay where you are,' she commanded.

'It's lonely up here,' he cajoled.

'Oh, you'll be all right. The night's still young, no doubt you can find one or other of your girlfriends to keep you company,' she said acidly as she opened the car door and got out. Charles hastily followed her. He grabbed her and held on firmly. She felt that familiar thrill surge through her at his touch; but this time there was another feeling over-riding it. A feeling of anger tinged with jealousy.

'What's the matter with you?' Charles cried. He was worried, he was losing his hold on her, she was slipping from his grasp; despite all his charm she was going to get away.

'Nothing now,' Calico said fixing her eyes glaringly on his. 'I've broken the spell,' she said triumphantly.

'Have you been drinking?' he asked. 'You're talking nonsense.'

'And that's your prerogative, you do it so well.'

'What, do what?' he asked bewildered.

'Talk nonsense. You open your mouth and it flows out in a stream: effusive, emotive, effluent.'

What is she on about? thought Charles. Women weren't for bandying words with; they were for laying flat on their back and enjoying. He was not into this intellectual thing, give him a body and he knew what to do with it. He could titillate their erogenous zones, and have a writhing mass of femininity panting for him no problem. When they started to talk too much he gave them the elbow. He was not interested in conversation with them, he could get that from his mates down the pub. 'Calico, why are you treating me like this? You know how much I think about you; how much I want you. Don't do this to me, don't walk away from me, I can't bear it,' he pleaded. He tried to hold her closer to him, to touch her body with his.

An odd feeling came over Calico as she looked at Charles under the glow of the street light. His face was still handsome, but his lovely smile transformed into a leer; the intense emotion she used to see in his deep brown eyes changed to lust; the caress in his voice she used to melt under sounded whining now; his face had become distasteful to her as she saw his real personality shine out through it.

'I should have done this the first time you kissed me,' she said in a seductive tone, looking at him levelly as she kneed him in the nuts and walked away. She threw a parting remark over her shoulder as he grovelled on the ground. 'It's a pity the damage isn't permanent. I'd deserve a medal then for my services to womankind.'

Chapter Fourteen

A Tragedy

> Who breathes, must suffer; and who thinks, must mourn;
> And he alone is bless'd who ne'er was born.
>
> Prior

Amy arrived at the Mansion House after lunch. The staff stayed to welcome her. Cook had saved her a meal. They all sat around the kitchen table chatting to make Amy feel relaxed and among friends, while she ate, or rather picked, at her meal.

'I saw the new Lord Mayor,' announced Cook. 'Nice gent, about my age, a widower, so I was told.'

'Hope he's nicer than the last one,' commented Susan.

'She always looked as though she had a bad smell under her nose, when she deigned to talk to you. Snobby cow.'

'Always done herself up well,' put in Vera.

'Her face and outer clothes yes,' agreed Grace, 'but you can't go by outward appearances. My mother used to be a personal maid to a really fine lady. She was always immaculately turned out, but she'd wear the same underwear for a fortnight.'

'So what you're saying is,' said Susan simplifying the matter, 'glamorous get-up covers dirty drawers.'

There was an odd noise; odd because no one had heard it for a long time, and had nearly given up hope of ever hearing it again; it was laughter, Amy's laughter. Amy had remembered the time she starched the Lord Mayor's underwear. A time she had been carefree, when she had joie de vivre and optimism for the future. If only she could turn the clock back, she would avoid that pop festival, then she would not meet John or anyone like him, and this nightmare she was in would never be. Her laughter turned to tears. She rushed out of the room. Calico followed her. 'I forgot it,' sobbed Amy. 'For a few seconds I forgot what happened to me. I was back at the Lord Mayor's banquet, the night before the pop festival. Then it all came flooding in on me again, the darkness came back.'

Calico knew no words to comfort Amy. She remained silent and held her while the tears flowed.

'There is one thing though,' sniffled Amy. 'I've started my period. So I don't have to worry about being pregnant.'

'That's a relief,' said Calico truthfully. She did not know what Amy could do if she had been pregnant. She had no advice at all. She did not like the idea of abortion, but it would do more harm to Amy if she went full-term with the pregnancy. It was not the child's fault how it was conceived. It was a moral dilemma, and Calico was glad it did not have to be faced any more.

'Dry your eyes Amy and go back to the others,' instructed Calico.

'I can't face them,' implored Amy.

'They understand you've been through an upsetting time. You can't hide from them forever. They ask you no questions, they don't pry. They're your friends, they take you as you are, because they care about you,' said Calico reassuringly. 'Come on, they've been good enough to give up their free time so you wouldn't be alone this afternoon.'

'You would still be here,' argued Amy.

'Yes, but I'm on duty. The Lord Mayor asked me to pack some of her clothes ready for her departure. Her term of office is up at the end of the week. She has to be gone by lunchtime on Sunday.'

'Oh! I see. Well it is good of them. All right, I'll return to the kitchen,' said Amy, dully.

The Lord Mayor was giving an end of term party on Saturday evening. The incoming Lord Mayor was invited so he could meet all the people he would be coming in contact with, when he took up his new appointment. There was a lot of preparation to be done for the event, and they were short-staffed. Mr Jukes had been promoted to head butler; a move which met with everyone's approval. (The posts of under-butler and parlourmaid were being advertised.) It was to be a buffet meal, which Cook dreaded, so many different dishes to prepare. There were mushroom and prawn vol-au-vents, crabmeat boats, assorted canapés, smoked salmon mousse, duck terrine, homemade paté and Melba toast, varieties of salads and their accompanying dressings, fruit-filled pavlovas, sherry trifles, profiteroles, cheesecakes, and gateaux. Everything had to be so dainty and decorative. It took ten times as much preparation as a sit-down four-course meal; ten times as much worry to calculate how much food was needed.

'Fiddly fart-assing things,' Cook would cry out in desperation as she wrestled with the delicacies, trying to hastily fit them on their platter before checking the meat in the oven, and the sauce for the vol-au-vents.

Every flat surface in the kitchen would be covered with bits of food. The staff would take their break standing up; fearful lest they should inadvertently destroy hours of painstaking care, by moving something to make room on the kitchen table. Cook was best left alone; unless she made a specific request for helping hands. They made sure Cook's bottle of sherry was only part full, and hid any other full bottles. Cook's definition of cooking sherry was not a cheaper variety used for culinary purposes but a drink to partake of while cooking, to relax the body under stressful conditions. While preparing a sit-down meal the sherry was consumed in moderation, but the older staff knew from experience that preparing a buffet meal was quite a different matter. Hence the aforementioned precaution.

Most of the Mansion House silver had been recovered. The larger pieces and the gold salver (which Mr Rolph had been leaving until last to steal, as it would have been the most noticeable), graced the dining room table on which the buffet was to be laid out. The dumb waiter trundled up and down laden with platters piled high with beef, gammon, pheasant, fresh salmon, and asparagus quiches: what a cornucopia; surely a feast that would do justice to the gods. The extravagance encompassed the liquid refreshment also: there was enough spirits and mixers crammed on to the wooden board covering the snooker table, to supply one of the city's public houses for a month. An abundance of wine covered the side tables in the dining room, and the refrigerator downstairs was overflowing with bottles of champagne for the toasts. The Lord Mayor and Corporation had spared no expense with the ratepayers' money on her leaving do.

Although Calico did not condone Mr Rolph's recent behaviour, and his attitude when he was employed at the Mansion House, she could begin to understand it. A person with a weak character could easily give in to temptation surrounded by people who spent the enforced contributions of others so wastefully and self-indulgently. Watching them spend public money so freely, Mr Rolph had only extended their generosity to cover himself and those he chose to favour.

Calico had been on duty all day. Amy had been sent to bed with a hot-water bottle. She had complained of severe period pains in the morning. Mr Jukes had advised her to have a few hours sleep, as he needed her to be recovered by the evening for the Mayor's leaving party. 'We're three staff short as it is,' he informed her. 'Grace's daughter is covering for Maria in the kitchen, but with a butler and a parlourmaid short the upstairs staff are thinly spread already.'

That evening Calico was stationed at the front door to let the guests in, and to direct the ladies upstairs to where Amy collected their coats from them. *The animal skins are out in force tonight*, thought Calico, *it must resemble a fur-trading post in the spare dressing room*. Then the ladies began to make their entrances, flowing down the wide staircase like something out of the pages of a glossy fashion magazine. Every one a posing clothes-horse. Evening gowns of every conceivable hue in silk, satin, brocade, lamé, velvet, lace, (no polyester or crimplene in sight), most of them one-off designs the cost of which would keep a family of four in comfort for a month. What a faux pas to arrive in the same dress as someone else (my dear, one would think I purchased my clothes from a chain store, or worse by mail order). Necks, ears, and wrists, dripping with jewels, real or imitation.

'Have we met? Your face seems familiar to me,' said the cultured voice of a particularly glamorous lady as she entered the hallway.

'No, I'm afraid not,' answered Calico politely, thinking that it was doubtful they would move in the same social circles.

'You do not recognise me at all?' she insisted. 'Of course it could have been before I lightened my hair a little. The sun bleached it when we were cruising in the Caribbean for a month.'

Calico shook her head. *That colour owes more to a bottle than to nature*, she thought. Calico studied the woman's face as she moved away from her. *I have seen her somewhere before, she's right; I know*, realised Calico, *she was the hostess at the party Tryphena took me to; thank goodness she didn't remember me. I'd better keep out of her way. Wonder how she got an invite? But there are so many hangers-on gathered together here, I suppose it's not that difficult.*

Calico noted that the waitresses did not look too pleased. She smiled to herself. With Mr Rolph gone they would miss out on their little perks. Mr Jukes was a happily married man, he did not require their attentions, he was not interested in anything they had to bargain with, his wife satisfied him. They would be going home empty-handed tonight. He did not give them cash for their taxi fare home either. He booked the taxis if requested, and the taxi firm sent in their account to the City Council for payment. Mr Jukes knew the waitresses used to arrange lifts home and pocket the taxi fares. They would only get paid for the work they did and no extras as far as he was concerned.

Calico was on her way downstairs to re-fill an ice-bucket and collect a couple of lemons, when a voice called after her, 'Excuse me poppet,' She stopped and looked in the direction of the voice. An oldish man with a scraping of grey hair and a thin pleasant face was addressing her. 'Could I come with you? I'm the new Lord Mayor, I'd like to see the staff who put in so much work behind the scenes.' 'Of course,' answered Calico. 'Follow me.'

He held on to the stair-rail as he slowly descended the steps after her. His body was thin and wirey, almost fragile, but bolt upright. Calico left him in the staff hallway.

'Would you wait here please,' she said politely, not wanting him to venture into the kitchen. She wanted to warn the others first. 'It would be better if I sent them out to meet you. It's always a bit chaotic in there when a function's in progress.'

'All right, thank you poppet,' he replied.

Calico told the first person she came across in the kitchen, that the new Lord Mayor would like to meet them and he was out in the hallway waiting. Knowing that the news would spread like a dry bracken blaze through the kitchen, from person to person. It did not take long before the kitchen resembled the Marie Celeste, and the staff were assembled in the hall. They formed a line, as they had seen people do when introduced to Royalty. The new Lord Mayor went along the line, having a word with each of them in turn. They introduced themselves to him, until he came level with Vera. They looked at each other. Vera had her mouth open, but no sound was forthcoming. He broke the silence between them. 'Is it Vera?' he asked and then answered himself. 'It is. How could I fail to recognise you; even after all this time. How are you? What have you been doing since we last met?'

'Walter,' was all Vera managed to contribute to the conversation.

He, realising Vera was disconcerted at the unexpected meeting, quickly said, 'It was nice to see you again. We'll catch up with our news another time,' and passed on to the next person. He said a general 'goodbye' and 'see you tomorrow' when he reached the end of the line, took his leave of them, and went upstairs to socialise with the guests.

When Calico returned upstairs, Mr Jukes asked her if she had seen Amy on her travels. Calico had to admit she had not seen her for a while. Mr Jukes sent her to find Amy to make sure she was all right. She tracked her down lying on the bed in the spare room. 'I still have bad period pains,' moaned Amy. 'So I lay down for a while to try to ease them.'

Calico reported back to Mr Jukes, who told her to tell Amy to go to bed if she felt that bad, they could manage now.

A lot of the guests were ready to depart having indulged in as much free food and drink as they could put away. The tailored evening suits and designer dresses were beginning to look a little strained along the seam lines. Several of the guests had quaffed too freely, and were becoming abusive to the others. Poor Mr Jukes did not know which one to persuade to go home first. He did not count being a bouncer as a prerequisite of butlering. Tact he had in abundance, but if they turned nasty he would be at a loss with strong-arm tactics. Luckily their respective partners saved the situation and hustled them homeward, leaving Mr Jukes to wipe the sweat from his brow, and breathe a big sigh of relief.

Mr Jukes told Calico she could go up to her room now. 'You've had a long tiring day and worked hard. I'll finish down here and round up the stragglers. We'll leave the clearing-up until tomorrow. I've asked the rest of the girls to come back in the morning. What with getting out one Lord Mayor and installing another, there will be plenty for us all to do. I've got a couple of interviews as well. The only time these people could attend was this Sunday,' Mr Jukes informed her.

Calico went upstairs. She called in on Amy to see if she felt better. Calico was pleased to see she was fast asleep and peaceful. Calico went straight to sleep; as people do after a hard day's toil. She did not even think about William's unanswered question. The days had been so full recently, she had not had time to sift through her thoughts about it and him. But he was being true to his word and not pressurising her; which must count as a big plus in his favour.

The next morning Amy was already in the kitchen preparing the Lord Mayor's breakfast, when Calico arrived there.

'How do you feel?' enquired Calico.

'Not too bad,' replied Amy. 'I felt guilty leaving you with the extra workload lately so I thought I would get up and do my share from now on.'

'Don't worry about that,' assured Calico. 'It's not your fault if you're not well.'

'My period is backward this time. I usually start off heavy the first few days, and then tail off; this time I started light and it's got heavier,' Amy remarked, frowning.

'Could be because it's an irregular one,' suggested Calico helpfully.

'That's what I put it down to,' agreed Amy. 'That's probably why my period pains got worse.'

Cook arrived then. 'Morning you two. Glad to see you're up and about Amy, still look peaky though,' she said cheerily.

Calico served the Lord Mayor and her consort with breakfast, their last meal in the Mansion House. 'You seem to be one of the stalwarts. Where do you live?' asked the Lord Mayor.

'In a village about twenty miles from here. My father's got a farm there,' answered Calico.

'That accounts for it, a farmer's daughter, made of stern stuff,' observed the Mayor. 'Comes from sturdy stock.' Calico scowled, she did not take kindly to the Lord Mayor's remarks. They sounded similar to her father's, when he was discussing the bloodlines of a pair of animals he was debating mating.

The rest of the staff arrived in dribs and drabs, and were put to work straight away so there was no time to chat. At breaktime it was as if the cork had been blown from a bottle of effervescent liquid. They had all subdued their curiosity for so long, that it now bubbled up and overflowed. Each wanted to ask the same question of Vera. 'How do you know Walter?' A row of expectant faces greeted Vera, as they waited for her answer.

'I was engaged to him, when I was a young girl,' she said at last, looking sad.

'We suspected as much,' the others agreed.

'How romantic,' said Susan wistfully. 'To meet up again after all this time.'

'And how convenient, him being a widower,' added Cook.

'What happened? Why didn't you marry him?' questioned Grace inquisitively.

'You don't have to tell them anything you don't want to, Vera. This lot won't let you have a private life; they niggle at it until they know more than all,' said Mr Jukes good-humouredly. 'Tell them to mind their own business.'

'It's no big deal,' stated Vera. 'We were engaged, and had agreed to marry the following year. Then Walter's firm sent him abroad. He was returning after six months so we could be married. And then I was going back with him until his contract expired,' Vera paused.

'What happened?'

'What stopped you?' cut in several voices at once.

'In the meantime,' continued Vera. 'my father died. My mother was in such a state I couldn't leave her. It would have been different if I was only moving a few miles away; but a few hundred miles away.'

'How sad.'

'What a shame.'

'But you didn't get married either?' said the others.

'No,' said Vera sadly. 'I wrote to Walter; I told him it wouldn't be fair to marry him, and not join him abroad, so I broke off the engagement. I felt my mother needed me for a while. When she'd recovered, then I would be free to marry Walter if he'd still have me. But Mother never got over the shock of losing her husband.'

'And you never saw Walter again until last night,' finished Susan.

'Did you never meet anyone else?' queried Grace.

'No. I didn't go out, I stayed at home and kept Mother company at first. Then as time went on I had nowhere to go. All the people I used to socialise with, were married and had families,' said Vera quietly. 'The years just seemed to roll on by.'

Grace and Susan looked at each other. They were both thinking the same thing. They thought their lives were pretty miserable, but they were not so bad compared to Vera's. They had husbands and families, they had something to show for their time on earth. Whatever they said and felt about them, they would not be without them, did not regret their existence.

'He rang me this morning,' announced Vera brightening.

'Walter?' asked Calico, stating the obvious.

'Yes. We're going out to tea this afternoon.'

'That's great. He's a fast worker,' they all chorused, smiling at her, immersed in hope for her. Amy got up from the table to take her cup and plate to the sink. There was a crash. The others looked around quickly to see what had happened. Amy was laid on the floor: she had passed out. Mr Jukes telephoned for an ambulance.

'That poor girl,' murmured Cook. 'Fate seems determined to give her a hard time; let's hope this is an end to it.'

'Yes,' agreed Susan. 'She ought to go for a two week holiday in the sun after this, to get her strength back before starting work again.'

Mr Jukes allowed Calico to travel in the ambulance with Amy who came round on the way to the hospital. The hospital staff thought it best to admit her anyway, as she still complained of severe stomach pains. The staff questioned her and the duty doctor examined her. They decided to give her a scan. There was no one available to do it on a Sunday so they would keep her in overnight and scan her first thing in the morning. Calico stayed with her for a while.

'I feel so weak and so frightened,' said Amy miserably. 'I haven't felt well since that awful night. As if my will was sapped out of me.'

'You'll be all right now Amy,' reassured Calico. 'I don't mean in your mind, how could you ever forget it. But physically, they'll sort you out in here and mend your body. Find out what's wrong.'

Amy smiled wanly. 'And that's what you believe?'

'Yes. God will get you out of this mess,' said Calico confidently. 'I'll leave you now, but I'll be back to see you tomorrow afternoon.'

When Calico arrived back at the Mansion House the other staff had gone home, except for Cook who had saved her a meal and waited for her return.

Calico relayed the news regarding Amy to her. Cook imparted her information, 'Mr Jukes has two people in his office. They've come about the parlourmaid job. Nice girls they look, quite normal.'

'Good,' replied Calico. 'We could do with some nice normal people here, after the last ones.'

'Wonder where they are now?' queried Cook.

'Who?' asked Calico acting dense.

'Mr Rolph, his son, Maria, and Sophia,' Cook amplified.

'Up to no good wherever they are,' said Calico, cynically.

'That's for sure,' laughed Cook.

Mr Jukes brought the interviewees into the kitchen. He introduced them and asked Cook if she would be kind enough to make tea for them all, as she was not officially on duty. Over tea and cakes, Cook and Calico started their subtle interrogation.

'Do you know each other?' began Cook.

'Yes, we travelled here together,' replied the younger girl. Her name was Ziglione. She was attractive, with big brown flashing eyes, a mane of thick black hair, and pouting lips.

'That's an unusual name you have,' commented Calico, not daring to pronounce it.

'My grandfather named me after his mother, he is Italian. He was in this country as a prisoner of war, met my grandmother, who is English, married her, and remained here ever since,' she explained. 'You can call me Ziggy.'

'It's a shame only one of you can have the job,' stated Cook.

'There are two posts advertised,' said the other girl, Joanne. Her blonde hair was cut very short, giving a severity to her face and her sharp pointed features, until she smiled, then she looked elfish and full of mischief. Ziglione and Joanne contrasted each other in every way.

'Yes,' agreed Cook, 'But only one's for a parlourmaid.'

'That's the job I'm applying for,' put in Ziggy.

'And I'm applying for the other job,' added Joanne.

'But it's for a man!' exclaimed Cook.

'It doesn't specify that,' countered Joanne.

'A butler is always male,' remonstrated Cook. 'Wherever I've worked they have been.'

'Why?' questioned Joanne.

'I don't know, because they always are I suppose,' answered Cook flustered.

'Tradition. No other reason. There is nothing a male butler can do that a female cannot. It doesn't require physical strength, which is the only advantage men have over women,' argued Joanne.

'You're right,' said Cook. 'The kitchen used to be a woman's preserve, now it's been invaded by male cooks, so why not female butlers?'

'I never even thought about it before,' admitted Calico. 'But there are a lot of jobs women can do equally as good as men.'

'Being a mere male,' put in Mr Jukes. 'I am now in somewhat of a quandary. Would my superiors approve of a female butler?'

'They had a female Lord Mayor,' retorted Calico.

'Yes, but that was not their choice, she was voted in by others,' replied Mr Jukes.

'I'm not asking you to employ me because I'm a woman,' stated Joanne. 'I'm asking you to look objectively at the qualifications and experience of candidates, regardless of their sex, and choose the person best suited to the position.'

'I can't do that,' said Mr Jukes with conviction.

'It seems very fair to me,' said Cook, realising after all these years, her ideas of the roles men and women took through life were preconceived from her mother, and her grandmother. She felt the stirrings of rebellion inside her. 'Why not give the girl a chance. At least consider her alongside the others as equals.'

'I've told you I can't do that,' repeated Mr Jukes. All four women chipped in with their remarks, and their opinion of Mr Jukes.

'Because,' shouted Mr Jukes above their clucking. 'Joanne is the only applicant so far.'

Mr Jukes chuckled into the silence that followed this statement.

'You rotter,' said Cook, they were all smiling now, 'you were having us on.'

'Well, you need to be teased now and then,' replied Mr Jukes. 'Women get so hysterical and bolshie when they've got a placard to wave, and a cause to support. You're so emotional.'

'Yes, but we have to behave like that to get things changed,' declared Joanne. 'We have to fight for things men take for granted as their birthright – their inheritance as a male member of the species. We have to inch our way along to gain an equal footing on the ground that men have been allowed to stand on for generations. Look at the struggle women had to get the vote.'

'Not all women feel that way,' observed Calico; thinking of her Gran, who had her husband firmly under her thumb. Gran nagged or sulked until she got her own way over everything. She did not need liberating, Granfer did.

'I'll wait until the last post Saturday,' said Mr Jukes to Joanne. 'If there are no other applicants by then the position is yours.' He turned his attention to Ziggy. 'I've others to interview for parlourmaid; I'll inform you either way, as soon as I've made a decision. Mr Jukes got up from his chair. 'I'm going over home for a few hours. I'll be back later to settle in the new Lord Mayor. Bye ladies,' he said taking his leave of them.

'What a nice man,' commented Ziggy. 'He seems like a real gent.'

'He is a pleasure to work for,' affirmed Cook.

'But then anything would have been an improvement on the last head-butler,' intimated Calico.

'Why, what was he like?' Ziggy wanted to know.

'He was a bit of a tyrant, that's all,' said Cook quickly, giving a silencing glance to Calico. It would not do to tell too many people what Mr Rolph had done. When they were working here, that was time enough to tell them about him. Joanne and Ziglione departed, Cook followed soon after, and Calico was left on her own. She began thinking about home.

It seemed ages since she last saw her parents, but it wasn't that long ago: it was because so much had happened at the Mansion House since the Christmas break. Being so short-staffed she could not be spared her day and a half off next week either. She had not seen William, being on duty most of the time. He had telephoned every day trying to arrange a time to see her, but they had not managed it so far. Her life seemed completely taken over by the Mansion House and its demands. She had wanted to visit Amy this evening, but she could not. She had to be on duty to look after the new Lord Mayor: draw his bedroom curtains, put a hot-water bottle in his bed, make him a milky bedtime drink. She did not enjoy her job any more. She was only a skivvy to others; resentment was creeping in. Over-tiredness, home-sickness, worry over Amy, the events of the past week, all were taking their toll on her, influencing her thinking. She telephoned the hospital before she went to bed. They told her they could not tell her anything until Amy had been for her scan, and to ring back in the morning after nine o'clock.

Mr Jukes had told Calico to have a lie-in the following morning; he would get the Lord Mayor's breakfast ready and lay the table. Calico came down for her breakfast at nine thirty. Cook asked her, 'How's Amy?'

'They didn't tell me last night. She's having a scan this morning, so they can tell me more when they get the results of it. I thought I'd ring about mid-morning, that should give them time to find out if there's anything wrong,' replied Calico.

'I'll telephone if you want,' offered Cook. 'Save you coming downstairs again before breaktime.'

'All right, thanks,' answered Calico gratefully. She was less worried about Amy now. After the scan the doctors would be able to sort out any problems.

Cook was in the staff hall as Calico came down to morning break. 'I've been trying to get through to the hospital. I keep getting engaged tones,' complained Cook, with her hand over the receiver.

'Oh, I'm through this time, it's ringing.'

Calico went into the kitchen to join the others around the table. They heard the 'ting' as Cook replaced the telephone receiver. She came slowly into the kitchen. Her face was white and her hands were trembling. Someone gave her a cup of tea, she could not hold it steady. The cup rattled against its saucer, slopping tea into it.

'She's dead!' exclaimed Cook.

'What,' they all said in one disbelieving voice.

'Amy's dead. The hospital told me she died in the night. They tried to contact her mother, but they were unable to reach her. They didn't know who else to contact,' said Cook, stunned.

'How can she be dead?' demanded Calico. 'She only went in for a scan.'

'She was pregnant, but it was an ectopic pregnancy. She haemorrhaged and died sometime in the night,' explained Cook sadly, tears filling her eyes.

'No, oh no. Poor Amy,' wailed Calico.

They all had tears flowing down their faces. Even the gardener found it difficult to blink them back. When Mr Jukes entered the kitchen he wondered what he had stumbled across. 'Whatever is the matter; all this weeping and wailing; have we run out of chocolate biscuits again?'

'Amy's dead,' they chorused through their sobs.

Chapter Fifteen

A Blow for Women

God saw that the pathway
Was getting hard to climb,
And so He closed your eyes
And whispered 'Peace be thine.'

Calico looked at the message she had put on Amy's wreath. The first wreath she had ever bought. This was another part in the painful process of growing up. People died who were not vague faces, distant ancient relatives you hardly knew, whose funeral was attended with the rest of the family, because it was expected of you. Amy was a friend, the person she had laughed with, talked with, shared experiences with; the first friend she had made away from home. Calico had to keep forcing back the tears as she went about her duties at the Mansion House. There were so many memories of Amy there. It was the same at breaktimes; they would chat for a while, then a chance remark would bring the conversation around to Amy.

They would all go silent, remembering, thinking of the tragedy that had befallen her.

Cook, usually such an honest woman, had taken to steaming open any envelopes that arrived at the Mansion House with handwritten addresses on them. She came to work earlier in the mornings, telling Calico to leave Mr Jukes's post on the kitchen table, and she would put it in the butler's office for her. While Calico was upstairs serving the Lord Mayor his breakfast. Cook was downstairs making her contribution to women's liberation. Rather late in life had she been awakened to it, but it must have been in her lying dormant. Any letters from applicants for the under-butler's position she pocketed to dispose of later. The rest she re-sealed and put on Mr Jukes's desk. Joanne would not have been at all pleased if she had known of Cook's actions on her behalf. The whole point of equality to her was that she was chosen for a job on her merit not by default. She did not mind a man procuring the job she was after, if he had more experience or better qualifications. What she objected to was a less experienced or unqualified man being chosen, because he was a man; or herself being overlooked simply because she was a woman.

Amy's funeral was a quiet affair at the local crematorium – her mother's decision. She could not afford the expense of a church burial she explained. Mr Jukes invited her back to the Mansion House, where Cook had prepared a funeral tea. Amy's mother accepted. 'I would like to meet the people who have been so kind to my darling Amy,' she effused. 'Taken so tragically from us. A wasted life, so much left to live for.' She dabbed at the corners of her eyes. The staff exchanged glances, all thinking much the same thing. Here was Amy's mother lamenting her tragic loss, as if Amy had been her whole world, instead of just a bit-player in it. We are all guilty of this, not taking enough notice of people we love while they are with us; only realising and regretting it when they are no longer there.

Amy's mother sat in a corner of the staff sitting room crying quietly. The staff sympathised with her. It is a hard heart that cannot be moved by another's grief. However badly she had treated Amy, she was paying for it now. They could tell she had loved her, she was just selfish and thoughtless in her attitude towards her. If only she had been made to realise how Amy felt before, then this tragedy could have been diverted.

Charles had joined the funeral tea. He managed to speak to Calico alone in the kitchen.

'You're a bitch, but I'm still crazy about you,' he said quietly, turning his flirtatious charms on her.

'Ditto,' replied Calico, 'But I'm not so gullible now as when I first met you.'

'Meet me then,' Charles urged, sensing a weakening.

'No Charles. I admit I find you physically exciting, but I don't like you as a person at all,' she concluded.

'You can use my body if it turns you on, I won't object. In fact you're getting me all excited at the idea of being your sexual plaything; any time, anyhow, anyway, baby, mm-mmm,' he caressed her with a drawling voice, put his arms around her pulling her in to him, smiling to himself at her seeming complacency. He did not think she was going to be this easy. He nuzzled her neck, as she wrapped her arms about him.

'You bring out the worst in me,' Calico murmured passionately, reaching behind his back; her fingers closed on what they had been seeking.

'Oh Charles,' she said breathlessly in his ear, deftly undoing the top button of his trousers with her free hand.

'Not here,' moaned Charles, 'In the ahhhhhh—'

'Let's see if that'll cool your ardour,' snapped Calico as she deposited a handful of ice-cubes inside his trousers. 'You think a few kisses and caresses from you, and women will lie down and beg you for it and be grateful. Well I want more than that. I want the person I make love with still there beside me in the cold light of day. Someone I can have a conversation with as a friend,' Calico called after him as he rushed past her furious at letting her dupe him a second time.

Tryphena entered the kitchen. 'Whatever's the matter with Charles? He rushed past me without a word. Have you been annoying him again?' she enquired.

He's been annoying me more like,' retorted Calico. 'It's his manner, "Here I am, come and get me."'

'He is handsome though, oozes charm, and he is a brilliant lay, best I've ever had; fulfils my physical needs whenever I get the urge. Oh! now I've shocked you,' said Tryphena, catching sight of the look that passed over Calico's face.

'No, not really,' replied Calico. 'It's just that I've never heard a woman say anything like that before, it was a surprise.'

'You're still a virgin, aren't you?' stated Tryphena. Calico turned her eyes downward, as though it was something to be ashamed to admit.

'I knew you were when Charles wasn't able to seduce you. You wouldn't have been able to resist him otherwise; he's so good at what he does,' said Tryphena matter-of-factly.

'I've got a lot to learn, haven't I?' declared Calico.

'Yes, but don't rush it. Wait until you find the right man for you and take precautions,' advised Tryphena. 'Remember what happened to Amy. She wasn't careful enough.'

'I'm not likely to ever forget it,' said Calico, the tears welling up in her eyes again.

'I thought Amy would have been smarter than to get herself pregnant,' commented Tryphena, haughtily. Calico regarded Tryphena through a watery veil.

Is that what she thinks? I suppose not knowing the whole story, she would come to that conclusion. Calico thought she ought to put the record straight. Amy had made her promise not to tell anyone about the rape; well, she had kept her promise. Now Amy was dead, as good as murdered. She did not want people to think badly of Amy; she did not want them to believe her death was self-inflicted by her own foolishness. Surely a promise to a dead person was not binding.

'It wasn't her fault,' hissed Calico quietly.

'Not entirely, no, it does take two,' quipped Tryphena.

'It wasn't her fault at all,' emphasised Calico.

'What are you saying?' questioned Tryphena.

'She was raped,' blurted out Calico.

Tryphena's eyes widened, she mouthed the word to herself, 'Oh God, no. How dreadful. I never guessed. Who? When? Poor Amy, to suffer in silence.'

'The night I told you Sophia had locked the door, and I went back down when she had gone to bed to unlock it for Amy.'

'You never told me. Who was it?' demanded Tryphena.

'Amy made me promise not to tell anybody. It was a chap called John, the one she met at the pop festival, and a chap named Silver,' revealed Calico.

'Didn't she go to the police?' asked Tryphena.

No. She didn't think they would believe her, seeing as she was in John's flat of her own free will, naked and in bed,' explained Calico.

'We'll get the bastards,' spat out Tryphena venomously.

'How? Amy's dead, there's no proof. She can hardly testify against them from the other side,' said Calico scathingly.

'They will regret what they did to Amy,' said Tryphena through clenched teeth, 'I can assure you.'

'You won't have them murdered?' asked Calico suddenly.

'Oh no! More subtle than that. We can't get them for rape, but we can get them on a drugs charge, and see to it that they're put away for a long time. Why should they be enjoying themselves and free, when Amy isn't,' concluded Tryphena.

'But how can we do that?' Calico could not comprehend.

'You let me worry about it. Just give me as much detail of their appearance as you can, and where they live. I have contacts in high places, and several useful bits of information at my disposal which could cause acute embarrassment to certain people, if they became common knowledge. Besides the majority of people do not condone rapists, so they will be sympathetic to my plans,' assured Tryphena.

'It's awkward. Two wrongs don't make a right,' hesitated Calico, 'but then what they did to Amy shouldn't be allowed to go unpunished.'

'They are evil, Calico, they victimise women, they need to be dealt with,' said Tryphena ominously, looking like an avenging angel. The determined set of her jawline, her face immobile as though carved out of stone, her eyes like chips of steely-blue ice. Calico, looking at her awesome features, did not doubt her. She almost, for a split-second, felt sorry for them. But when she thought of Amy, they deserved everything they got, she decided.

'I must make a note never to get on the wrong side of you, without first procuring a crucifix and some garlic,' she stated.

Tryphena's stern face broke up at this, she could not hold back a smile. 'You need not bother with them. Your inherent goodness alone would be enough to make me feel sick and weak.'

'Thanks a lot,' returned Calico looking a bit hurt by Tryphena's tone.

'Oh! Don't get me wrong. I'm not knocking it. In fact I'm jealous of it,' Tryphena retorted.

'Jealous?' repeated Calico astonished.

'Yes. You're never going to let yourself get into awkward situations, that lead to misery and destruction,' explained Tryphena.

'But I nearly did,' admitted Calico, 'With Charles.'

'Yes, nearly being the operative word to underline my point,' stressed Tryphena. 'When it came to the crunch that's what you gave him.' Tryphena laughed.

'It was mean of me, it was a spur-of-the-moment action,' said Calico rather ashamed at hurting Charles. 'This time I was more subtle.'

'He got what he deserved. It may take a long time, but you always get back what you give out. The same for those two apologies for men, who sent Amy to her death,' snarled Tryphena.

'And what about Amy?' ventured Calico quietly, 'She didn't deserve what she got.'

'No. I have to admit I've no answer to that. Perhaps she was one of the unfortunate people, who inadvertently get snared in the evil web wound around the actions of others,' suggested Tryphena. 'The innocent bystanders in life.'

Several of the staff appeared in the kitchen, finishing further conversation between Calico and Tryphena. The funeral tea was coming to an end, and they were helping to clear it away. Amy's mother entered to say goodbye to Calico. 'I wish I'd been a better mother to her. I feel it's all my fault. I should've tried harder with her,' she said. Calico did not contradict her. She knew that was what Amy's mother wanted; someone to say she was not to blame, to take the feeling of guilt from her. Calico felt sorry for her, but she could not bring herself to say something to absolve her. Amy's mother may not have been directly responsible for her death, but she was responsible for Amy's unhappy childhood which made her seek solace and affection elsewhere, and led ultimately to her destruction.

'Goodbye and thank you for coming,' Calico said politely in a cold formal voice.

Amy's mother searched Calico's face for some sign of friendliness in it; finding none she said, 'Goodbye Calico. Thank you for being Amy's friend.'

'I don't need thanking for that,' replied Calico sharply, 'It was a pleasure.'

When all the staff had departed, Calico sat quietly in the kitchen, contemplating. She could not stay. She would never feel comfortable here again. Amy was dead; Tryphena had moved out; Charles would continue to 'try it on' and make her feel awkward; Cook would be retiring soon; almost everything had changed during the year she had worked at the Mansion House, thought Calico. She did not like the people who employed her: not Mr Jukes, he was nice; but the Lord Mayor's secretary was full of his own self-importance, and the council members and their respective partners. The majority of them who were invited to the Mansion House banquets were arrogant self-centred hypocrites. They had clawed their way up to high positions and wealth, and now looked down with distaste at all the others floundering beneath them. Money was their god; with money all things are possible, well all the things that matter, the status symbols, were possible so they believed.

Calico had not been brought up to think this way. Their attitudes went against the grain for her. When she waited on them her body would go tense, her teeth would clench, and her eyes would fill with loathing; she had to fight against her inner feelings to make herself be pleasant to these people as it was what she was paid to do. It made her feel a hypocrite, suppressing her rebellious feelings and going against her conscience. She could do it no longer she decided. Tomorrow she would give in her notice. Mr Jukes was still interviewing for parlourmaids, so it should not inconvenience him unduly.

Mr Jukes tried to persuade Calico to reconsider when she informed him of her decision.

'Calico I wish you would stay. You're a hard worker, an excellent time-keeper, kind, cheerful, loyal, efficient, honest, steady, reliable, and everyone likes you,' listed Mr Jukes, 'You're just what this place needs.'

'That's why I have to go,' declared Calico.

'I don't understand,' replied Mr Jukes mystified.

'If I am all those things you say, then I want to remain that way. If I stayed here I'm afraid I would change and become like others here,' explained Calico.

'I've been here five years. It hasn't changed me,' said Mr Jukes feeling a little insulted by her remark.

'No I didn't mean you, Mr Jukes. You have your wife and children practically on the doorstep. You have breaktimes, lunchtimes, dinner times, and most evenings with them; that's your home, not the Mansion House. It's when you live here, and spend most of your time at this place, that it can change you. I've got this claustrophobic feeling, I've got to get out of this place,' explained Calico further. Mr Jukes looked puzzled.

'You know that feeling you get when you don't want to do a certain thing,' continued Calico, 'You don't know why, you just have an awful dread in the pit of your stomach about it.' Calico tried to clarify her earlier words without success.

Mr Jukes apparently had never suffered such acute agonies in his life. He frowned at her; maybe he was wrong in his assessment of her. She was not making much sense at the moment. 'If you feel that strongly about going there is nothing I can say to change your mind. But would you consider staying until Ziglione has settled in?' asked Mr Jukes.

'She got the job then. Of course I will. What about Joanne?' questioned Calico.

'Seeing as I have received no further applications for the position of under-butler, I've kept my word and given the position to her,' Mr Jukes informed Calico, 'It's very odd though. I would have thought more people would have been interested in the post, especially with all the perks that go with it.'

Calico took her leave of Mr Jukes, and went in search of Cook to tell her the news. Cook did not seem surprised when Calico imparted her recently gathered information to her.

'First round to women's rights,' said Cook, with an odd glint in her eyes and her fist clenched in the air. Calico did not have time to elaborate further on Cook's strange reaction as just then Vera entered the kitchen, looking all pink and flustered. They turned their attention to her.

'I-I-I'm getting married,' she stammered excitedly.

'Vera I am pleased for you!' exclaimed Calico.

'Yes, that's wonderful news,' ejaculated Cook.

'To Walter?' enquired Calico.

'Yes. I'm so happy. I never thought I'd ever see him again. Let alone get a second chance with him. Our feelings haven't changed, after all this time. I'm happy now, but I do feel regret for all those wasted years,' babbled Vera.

'What about your mother?' asked Cook.

'I'm putting her in a private nursing home. She'll be well cared for there. I'm selling the house to pay for it, and moving in with Walter. I sacrificed my happiness for her once, she can't expect me to do it a second time,' said Vera defiantly.

'Good for you,' cheered Cook. 'Break those maternal chains and start to live your own life.'

Calico thought Cook had finally flipped, the odd remarks she was coming out with this morning.

Cook had not lost her senses, in fact she had regained them. Nothing in her life had changed for years. She had looked after her mother until her death. She had lived in the same small flat all her life. She had been employed at the Mansion House for the past twenty years. Like Vera, she was having regrets. Nothing of importance had ever happened to her. Now she was nearing retirement she took stock of her situation. She could see a different world emerging; where women would play an equal role to men, and she wanted to be part of it. She was going to burn her bra and loosen her stays. Well not literally, it would be too much of a shock for her body when all that flesh met up, she had kept it separate for years; but metaphorically.

'I'll have a ready-made family,' said Vera cheerfully. 'He has two married daughters, and four grandchildren. They visit him often. I hope they won't resent me.'

'They should be pleased their father has found someone to share his old age with, and who makes him happy,' said Cook sensibly.

'I hope so,' sighed Vera.

'Now don't go finding things to worry about that might lead you to change your mind about marrying him. If they're decent people and have their father's interests at heart, they'll accept you,' assured Cook.

'Yes, I suppose so,' said Vera, not totally convinced. 'Don't tell the others please. I shouldn't really have told you two yet, but I'm so excited I had to let it out.'

Vera went on her way humming to herself.

Ziglione and Joanne arrived that evening. Joanne was anxious to install herself in the Mansion House as soon as possible; in case Mr Jukes had a change of heart under pressure from his superiors. They asked Mr Jukes if they could share the housekeeper's suite. Mr Jukes answered, 'I'm afraid I can't allow it. It would not be fitting for the under-butler and a parlourmaid to room together. Being a female butler, you can't be treated differently from your male counterpart. You would not expect me to allow a male butler and a female parlourmaid to share a room – unless of course they were married.' He smiled smugly.

'Touché,' scowled Joanne disappointed.

It would be pleasant to have company again, thought Calico. It was lonely for her when the daytime staff went home. Ziggy and Jo were friendly towards her, but they spent all of their free time together. Calico understood that they were good friends, but she felt it would be nice if they included her in their outings sometimes. Then one day she was in the kitchen with Ziggy, when Charles entered.

Charles still wanted Calico, she made him feel like no one else ever had before. He enjoyed his sex life, but imagined to himself the heightened sensual pleasure of making love to someone you wanted like crazy, who could drive you senseless with your desire of them, to be lost in the ecstasy of their very presence. He had a dull ache inside caused by his longing for that moment. He suddenly noticed Ziggy. He decided to chat her up, perhaps that would make Calico jealous, and she would realise what she would be missing. 'Hello,' he fixed her with his sexy look. 'Another new parlourmaid, and another good-looker too. I'm Charles, the Mayor's chauffeur.'

'Hello Charles, I'm Ziggy. Pleased to meet you,' she said, offering him her hand to shake. Charles took hold of her hand, raised it to his lips, and kissed it. Keeping his eyes on hers all through the performance.

Calico watched the scene out of the corner of her eye. She thought about warning Ziggy to be careful of Charles, but it might sound like sour grapes on her part. Besides Ziggy had been out in the world for a while. She was not like the naive country lass Calico had been when she first encountered Charles. No doubt Ziggy could take care of herself.

'You must have lots of boyfriends. I bet you drive them wild,' Charles continued his chatting up.

'No, I don't actually,' replied Ziggy.

'But you're such a fine figure of a woman, you could drive me wild,' drawled Charles, and added, 'Any time.'

'No I couldn't,' answered Ziggy, emphatically.

'Oh, believe me you could,' insisted Charles looking at her, his eyes half-closed, his lips slightly parted, his hand on his hip in what he believed to be a sexy pose. Surely she could not resist him.

'You're not my type,' Ziggy said nonchalantly.

Charles straightened up and opened his eyes wide in surprise. 'What is your type then?' he demanded sarcastically.

'Women,' she replied simply and walked out of the kitchen, leaving him to stare open-mouthed after her.

Calico was trying to suppress her laughter, making odd snorting noises in her attempt. She gave up and giggled out loud. Poor Charles was not having much luck lately with women. This was the third time Calico had seen him lost for words. She could not resist a jibe. 'What Charles, nothing to say, and you usually so eloquent,' she teased.

Charles glowered at her, 'I don't know what's happened to women nowadays, different breed altogether. Where's all the sweet gentle females gone?'

'You've had your day, you're out of time now Charles. Charm and physical good looks aren't enough, the majority of us don't swoon over a cad any more. We've got realistic. Men don't figure so largely in our lives, they are not the be all and end all of it. We can strike out on our own now, we don't have to hang on to your coat-tails to get us through. Don't worry, you won't become extinct, we're rather fond of you. We'll treat you exactly the same as you've been treating us all these years.'

Charles, still glowering, walked out. Calico continued laughing, she had not laughed for a while; now she had started she could not stop, it had taken hold of her. The tears rolled down her face as she giggled merrily. The sound of the telephone ringing cut into her mirth. She wiped her eyes and went to answer it.

'Hello Calico.'

'Hello William.'

'Are you visiting home this week at all?' he asked.

'No, but I'm going home this weekend,' she replied.

'Shall I pick you up from there?' he offered.

'No, you needn't do that, but will you meet me at the bus stop Saturday afternoon,'

'What time?' he enquired.

'About four thirty,' she answered.

'I can't sorry, I'll be milking,' he apologised.

'Please. It's important,' she begged.

'All right, I'll get someone to cover for me,' he agreed.

'Thanks,' she sounded relieved.

'What's it all about?' he questioned.

'I'll tell you when I see you. Take care William.'

'And you. I miss you Calico.'

'Bye William.'

'Bye Calico.'

All her goodbyes being said, Calico, travelling home on the bus for the last time, reflected on all that had happened since she took that other bus journey. The one that had taken her away from her innocence, and put her on the road to adulthood. She thought of Tryphena and Amy, Charles, Mr Rolph, Sophia and Maria; Mr Jukes, Cook, Vera, Susan, and Grace. The Lord Mayor and her consort: all the people who had weaved through her tapestry of life. Who had altered her ideas, added to her experiences, helped in her maturing process. She may not have liked them all, but she was richer for having known each one of them.

Her heart leapt at the sight of William, she had that odd sensation in the pit of her stomach. She smiled, she did feel more for him than friendship she decided. William helped her down with her cases. He set her luggage on the pavement.

'You've got a lot of luggage for a weekend visit,' observed William.

'I'm not visiting just for the weekend,' she replied.

'You mean,' began William grinning broadly, unable to contain his pleasure; Calico cut him short.

'I'm home to stay.' The relief of being on home territory, coupled with the emotional drain of the past year, and the feeling of wanting to be sheltered from the outside world for a while, all contributed to Calico's next statement. 'The answer to your question is yes, William. I will become engaged to you.'

Where she went from here Calico did not know, but she would worry about that another day. At the moment this was what she wanted.

'Oh Calico,' breathed William. He put his arms around her waist and held her tightly to him. She wrapped her arms around his neck with equal firmness. They clung to each other, their eyes closed, feeling the merging of their bodies, the emotions surging through them, the happiness invading them. A precious moment to be preserved for life.